Samuel French Acting Edition

The Princess and the Goblin

by Stuart Paterson

From the Book by
George MacDonald

SAMUELFRENCH.COM   SAMUELFRENCH.CO.UK

FOR PRODUCTION ENQUIRIES

UNITED STATES AND CANADA
Info@SamuelFrench.com
1-866-598-8449

UNITED KINGDOM AND EUROPE
Plays@SamuelFrench.co.uk
020-7255-4302

Each title is subject to availability from Samuel French, depending upon country of performance. Please be aware that *THE PRINCESS AND THE GOBLIN* may not be licensed by Samuel French in your territory. Professional and amateur producers should contact the nearest Samuel French office or licensing partner to verify availability.

Please refer to page 79 for further copyright information.

THE PRINCESS AND THE GOBLIN was premiered at Dundee Repertory Theatre on November 26, 1993 (running until the January 6, 1994) with the following cast:

PRINCESS IRENE . . . . Pauline Lockhart

NURSE LOOTIE/BANSHEE/SLY . . . . Carol-Ann Crawford

CROWN PRINCE KRANKL . . . . Richard Clews

KING COB/FATHER/CAPTAIN OF THE GUARD . . . . Eric Barlow

QUEEN MAM/MOTHER/SLY . . . . Irene MacDougall

KING-PAPA/FANNON . . . . Steven Hogan

GREAT GRANDMOTHER . . . . Kay Gallie

CURDIE PETERSEN . . . . David Tennant

Director - Hugh Hodgart
Designer - Gregory Smith
Music - Alan Penman
Lightning - Neil Goodwill

THE PRINCESS AND THE GOBLIN has subsequently been performed at The Royal Lyceum in Edinbugh and has had second productions at both Dundee Repertory Theatre and Edinburgh's Royal Lyceum. It has also been performed by Northern Stage at Newcastle Playhouse and at The MacRobert Centre Theatre in Stirling.

CAST OF CHARACTERS

PRINCESS IRENE

NURSE LOOTIE

PALACE-GUARD

CROWN PRINCE KRANKL, a goblin

KING COB, a goblin

QUEEN MAM, a goblin

KING-PAPA

GREAT-GRANDMOTHER

SLY, a goblin-creature

CURDIE PETERSEN

FATHER, Curdie's father

FANNON, a young dragon

MOTHER, Curdie's mother

CAPTAIN OF THE GUARD

BANSHEE, a witch

Possible doubling for a cast of 8:

KING COB/FATHER/CAPTAIN OF THE GUARD

LOOTIE/BANSHEE/SLY

QUEEN MAM/MOTHER/SLY

KING-PAPA/FANNON/PALACE-GUARD

(**SLY** is non-speaking, should wear a full face-mask, and can therefore be played at different times by different actors.)

ACT ONE

Scene One

(Night. The gardens of The King's Palace. The moon and stars shine brightly.)

(Enter **PRINCESS IRENE** *at a run. She is barefoot, in her nightdress.)*

IRENE. I've escaped! I'm free! *(moodily)* Wherever I go a guard goes too, and I am never without my nurse! How wonderful to be on my own.

VOICE. *(from off)* Irene! Where are you? Show yourself!

IRENE. Why can they never leave me alone?

(Enter **NURSE LOOTIE** *with a well-armed* **PALACE-GUARD**.*)*

LOOTIE. *(angrily)* Come inside, Irene! This minute!

IRENE. Always telling me what to do! Why am I never allowed out under the stars?

LOOTIE. Your father the king forbids it.

IRENE. But why?

LOOTIE. Because it's dangerous, that's why!

IRENE. Go away, Nurse Lootie. How can anything so beautiful be dangerous?

LOOTIE. At night all kinds of creatures crawl up from the darkness to enjoy the smooth lawns of the palace gardens.

IRENE. You make up stories to frighten me.

LOOTIE. I've no time for stories! Now, you'll come with me, without another word.

IRENE. Of course, you're right, Nurse Lootie. *(walks meekly to her* **NURSE***)*

LOOTIE. That's more like it.

(Suddenly **IRENE** *swerves and runs off.)*

The little monkey! *(to the* **GUARD***)* After her! Catch her, catch her.

*(***LOOTIE** *exits with* **GUARD** *in pursuit.)*

(Enter **THE GOBLINS, CROWN PRINCE KRANKL, KING COB** *and* **QUEEN MAM**, *like thieves.* **KRANKL** *and* **COB** *are barefoot, and they have no toes on their feet.* **MAM** *wears enormous shoes made of granite.)*

(thunder and lightning)

KRANKL. Hear how the sky shakes with fear at our coming into their world!

KING COB. The goblins are up!

QUEEN MAM. The goblins are out!

GOBLINS. *(in unison, to themselves)* Ssssh! The soldiers will hear us.

KRANKL. I hate all humans! How I long to hurt and torment them.

QUEEN MAM. And so you shall, Prince Krankl, so you shall.

KRANKL. Oh Mother – the opinion they have of themselves! Look how they have built their palace halfway to the moon!

KING COB. It is nothing to the great goblin palace we have carved beneath the mountain.

QUEEN MAM. Where you are King.

KING COB. And where you are Queen.

KRANKL. How dare they live above us when we are their betters in every way? Tell me, Mother, Father – how may I hurt them? Tell me quickly!

QUEEN MAM. My dear Prince Krankl, you may burn their barns.

KRANKL. *(closing his eyes in pleasure)* Yes, more!

KING COB. Poison their water!

KRANKL. Yes, more!

KING COB. Steal their sheep and cattle!

KRANKL. More, I tell you!

QUEEN MAM. *(more quietly, in his ear)* Steal their children.

KRANKL. *(his eyes springing open)* Oh yes! I hate their children worst of all.

KING COB. With their pretty eyes and happy smiles!

QUEEN MAM. They make me want to be sick!

KRANKL. To steal away a child…What joy! I must find a child! Now, now, now!

QUEEN MAM. But where, my sweet?

KING COB. There are none to be found.

KRANKL. *(sniffing the air)* What's that horrible smell?

QUEEN MAM. What smell?

KRANKL. Foof! *(holds his nose)* Are you sure you haven't, you know…?

KING COB. Of course we haven't.

QUEEN MAM. Don't be ridiculous. *(sniffs)* But wait – I'd know that smell anywhere. *(rounds on* **AUDIENCE***)* Children!

KRANKL AND KING COB. *(in unison)* Where?

QUEEN MAM. *(pointing.)* There!

> *(All three advance on* **AUDIENCE***.)*

KRANKL. Let me at them!

KING COB. *(to* **AUDIENCE***)* Smelly, revolting little brats!

QUEEN MAM. *(to* **AUDIENCE***)* Never forget –

GOBLINS. *(chanting, in unison)* We're bigger, we're braver, we're better than you! We're bigger, we're braver, we're better than you! Oh yes we are!

AUDIENCE. Oh no, you're not!

GOBLINS. *(in unison)* Oh yes we are!

AUDIENCE. Oh no, you're not!

KRANKL. We'll teach them a lesson! We'll steal away a child. *(Points into* **AUDIENCE***.)* It might be you, or you, or you, or, who knows, it might even be – *(a sudden jabbing finger)* you!

QUEEN MAM. Hush, my son – someone is coming.

KING COB. *(terrified)* S-s-soldiers!

KRANKL. *(looking off)* No, Father, it is a child, a pretty little child.

QUEEN MAM. Quickly, then, hide – and we shall take it by surprise!

KRANKL. Yes! We will take it down under the ground!

QUEEN MAM. Hide, I tell you!

(They hide.)

(Enter **PRINCESS IRENE.** *)*

IRENE. *(gazing up into the sky)* How lovely the stars are… They sparkle like precious stones…

LOOTIE. *(angrily, from off)* Irene! Stop hiding and come back here! I'm warning you!

IRENE. *(shouting off)* And I'm warning you! Leave me alone! I'll come outside if I want to!

*(***KING COB, KRANKL** *and* **QUEEN MAM** *come out of hiding, holding up a large black sack.)*

(Enter **NURSE LOOTIE** *with a well-armed* **PALACE GUARD.** *The* **GOBLINS,** *unseen, dive back into hiding.)*

LOOTIE. You're coming with me, girl! I won't tell you again.

IRENE. I'll stay where I am, thank-you very much.

LOOTIE. *(splutters with rage, controls herself)* The goblins will have your bones, by and by, and you will have only yourself to blame.

IRENE. *(scornfully)* Goblins! You won't frighten me.

(a distant rumble of thunder.)

LOOTIE. A storm is on the way. *(shivers)* You'll catch cold.

IRENE. *(breathes deeply)* What lovely air…When the rain comes I will let it soak me to my skin…

LOOTIE. I've heard enough! *(brandishes her stick)* You'll do what you're told!

IRENE. *(running)* You'll have to catch me first!

*(***LOOTIE** *chases her, shouting angrily, until the* **GUARD** *seizes* **IRENE** *and sweeps her up into his arms.)*

IRENE. How dare you! Put me down, put me down!

LOOTIE. To the palace, my girl, and let's have no more of your nonsense! To the palace!

(Exeunt NURSE LOOTIE *and* THE GUARD, *carrying* PRINCESS IRENE.*)*

*(*KING COB, PRINCE KRANKL *and* QUEEN MAM *come out of hiding.)*

KRANKL. Her eyes…and did you hear her? *(mimics* IRENE*)* "How lovely the stars are…What lovely air."

QUEEN MAM. I'll be sick!

KRANKL. She must be taught that the world is ugly and cruel…But her eyes, Father, did you see her eyes?

KING COB. They shine with a thousand dreams of happiness! Her beauty must be destroyed lest she make us dream too.

QUEEN MAM. Goblins never dream! They know better!

KING COB. We know that dreams hurt more than anything because dreams can never come true.

KRANKL. To take her dreams away…Oh, the joy of it! I must steal her and take her down with me into darkness! I must! I must!

KING COB. Be patient, my son.

QUEEN MAM. Wait your time, and she will surely be yours.

*(*QUEEN *and* KING *vanish underground.)*

KRANKL. Then Prince Krankl will watch, and he will wait. Do you hear me, little Irene? Wander out again among the stars and the goblins will have you for their own. I have sworn it! *(goes underground)*

Scene Two

*(**PRINCESS IRENE**'s nursery bedroom in the palace. The chandeliers are lit. Outside the wind blows and whistles.)*

*(Enter **PRINCESS IRENE** and **NURSE LOOTIE**.)*

LOOTIE. *(clapping her hands)* Back into bed, my girl, it's very late! Hurry, now!

IRENE. I want to go outside again and see the stars.

LOOTIE. You can see the stars anytime you like! Your father the king has had your ceiling painted all blue with stars in it. It is more like the sky than the sky itself.

IRENE. No! Now that I've seen the real stars I won't look at my ceiling ever again! I'm bored! I'm bored! I'm bored!

LOOTIE. You have the most beautiful toys in all the world. How can you be bored?

IRENE. I have a very great deal to become bored with, and you very little, so it's impossible for you to understand.

LOOTIE. *(furious)* What you need is a good…*(brandishes her stick, overstretches)* Oh, my poor old bones.

IRENE. Nurse Lootie, do your bones hurt?

LOOTIE. *(self-pityingly)* Oh yes, how they ache.

IRENE. Poor old Lootie, how selfish I've been. You must sit down and rest. *(takes her by the arm)*

LOOTIE. Oh yes, so I must.

*(Enter **KING-PAPA**, unseen by **IRENE** or **NURSE LOOTIE**.)*

IRENE. *(leads **LOOTIE** to chair)* Sit down, dear old nurse.

LOOTIE. You're a good girl when you try…Thank you…

*(**LOOTIE** sits, **PRINCESS IRENE** pulls her chair away, and **LOOTIE** screams as she falls to the ground in an undignified heap.)*

KING-PAPA. *(very loud)* Irene!

*(**IRENE** starts with fear.)*

What kind of way is this to behave!

LOOTIE. *(struggling in a ridiculous fashion)* Help, I can't get up!

IRENE. Father! How you made me jump!

KING-PAPA. I'll make you jump, girl, have no fear of that!

IRENE. She's not hurt. *(pulls* **NURSE LOOTIE** *to her feet)* See... She's as tough as an old boot.

KING-PAPA. Irene!

IRENE. You're alright now, nursie, aren't you? *(slaps her a few times)*

LOOTIE. I feel dizzy...I think I'm going to faint...

IRENE. Then sit down. *(pushes her hard, and she falls back into the chair)* There, that's better, isn't it?

LOOTIE. Everything's going round and round...

IRENE. Oh be quiet, and put your head between your knees. *(pushes her head down)*

KING-PAPA. You are a very rude and spoiled little girl!

IRENE. If I'm spoiled then someone must have done the spoiling!

KING-PAPA. Don't answer back!

IRENE. Don't shout at me!

LOOTIE. I do everything I can, Your Majesty, but you see how she is.

IRENE. Leave me alone!

LOOTIE. She's completely out of control!

KING-PAPA. I'm very angry with you, Irene! Do you hear me? You're not the girl I remember at all! You've grown self-ish and rude and...Irene, there are tears in your eyes!

IRENE. I hate to cry...I hate it! *(cries)*

LOOTIE. That's the way! She'll feel all the better for a good cry.

> *(**IRENE** cries harder and runs to her **FATHER** who embraces her.)*

KING-PAPA. Leave us, Nurse Lootie.

LOOTIE. Straight to bed and she'll be as right as rain in the morning.

KING-PAPA. Goodnight, Nurse Lootie.

LOOTIE. Goodnight, Your Majesty. *(curtsies and exits)*

KING-PAPA. *(gently)* Come to your bed...There are times when even a princess must do as she is told.

*(**KING-PAPA** lifts her up, carries her to bed. A rumble of thunder and outside the rain begins to pour down.)*

The storm has broken. *(puts her into bed)* You can sleep safe and warm in your feather-bed...But listen to the rain...It's pouring down like water from a full sponge.

IRENE. That's what my mother used to say...Do you miss her too?

KING-PAPA. Yes, all the time.

IRENE. Sometimes I get angry with her for not being here any more.

KING-PAPA. *(smiling)* You silly girl. She didn't die on purpose.

IRENE. *(laughing)* I know that, but all the same I wish she'd been clever enough not to die.

KING-PAPA. You must be brave and forgive her.

IRENE. I'll try, Father.

KING-PAPA. Good girl...In the morning I must go on my travels again, so that all the people may see their king.

IRENE. Don't go.

KING-PAPA. You know I must, and you must stay inside where it's safe and learn to be kinder to your nurse. There needs to be a big improvement in your behaviour! Do you hear me?

IRENE. *(sleepily)* Yes, Father...

KING-PAPA. Then go to sleep, Irene.

IRENE. Goodnight, Father.

KING-PAPA. *(kisses her)* Go to sleep.

*(**KING-PAPA** goes)*

IRENE. *(starting awake)* Don't go, please stay...Gone... *(dreamily)* But listen to the rain...Outside great brown streams will be tumbling down the mountainside... Tumbling and tumbling...It must be so beautiful... *(sits up)* How can anyone anywhere ever sleep? If I cannot explore outside the palace then I will explore inside. *(gets out of bed)* There are a hundred great halls, and if you climb the narrow stairs from the kitchens you come to the attic rooms…*(closes her eyes)* There are so many rooms no-one has been inside all of them… *(A clock strikes somewhere deep in the palace.)* It's the easiest thing to get lost here…utterly lost. *(Her bed vanishes, as it might in a dream.)* And there is no sound except the trampling of the rain on the roof…*(tearful)* It's so lonely and I'll never find my way out…I've looked and looked for the stairs down, but there is only a stair that goes up, a little stair of worm-eaten oak, up and up into the endless rooms where the white birds make their nests in the rafters…*(A gentle humming sound replaces the sound of the rain.)* What's that sound? It's like the buzzing of a bee…I am too afraid to look…But I am lost and I must look, I must…

*(She turns and sees a beautiful white-haired **OLD LADY** spinning at her wheel. **IRENE** starts back in fear and wonder. The **OLD LADY** works by the light of a bright orb that hangs in the air above her head, like her own little moon.)*

OLD LADY. Come in, my dear, I am very glad to see you. Don't be afraid. Come here, and let me look at you.

*(**IRENE** goes bravely to her.)*

Your face is streaked like the back of a zebra. Have you been crying?

IRENE. Yes.

OLD LADY. Why, child?

IRENE. Because I was lost.

OLD LADY. *(licking a hankerchief and wiping **IRENE**'s face)* Well, you have to be lost if you want to find yourself? Isn't that right?

IRENE. My mother has gone away and left me.

OLD LADY. Your mother is dead, I know, but her love for you will never die. That will live inside you for ever and ever.

IRENE. Who are you?

OLD LADY. My name is Irene.

IRENE. But that's my name!

OLD LADY. I know, but I had it first and you were named after me. I am your great-great-grandmother.

IRENE. What's that?

GREAT GRANDMOTHER. I am your father's mother's father's mother.

IRENE. Father's mother's father's…Oh, I can't follow that at all!

GREAT GRANDMOTHER. Yes, but that's no reason why I shouldn't say it. You were left in my care, and I have come to help you. *(finishes wiping* **IRENE***'s face)* There, that's better now, isn't it?

IRENE. Yes, thank-you. *(looking around)* What a beautiful room…And your dress, and your silver hair…You even have your own little moon. I wish I could bring my nurse to see it.

GREAT GRANDMOTHER. Lootie could look and look and still she would never see us.

IRENE. But why?

GREAT GRANDMOTHER. Some people have two good eyes, but are blind all the same. And even if for one second she did see us here, she would rub her eyes, shake her head and say it was all a dream.

IRENE. *(laughing, rubbing her eyes, shaking her head)* But why can I see when she can't?

GREAT GRANDMOTHER. Like a true princess you have wonder in your heart.

IRENE. Wonder?…But I'm not allowed to leave the palace. It's a very silly rule.

GREAT GRANDMOTHER. Yes, I quite agree.

IRENE. No-one has ever agreed with me before.

GREAT GRANDMOTHER. *(laughing)* It is very wrong to keep you prisoner here.

IRENE. Yes! I'm sure my mother would never have wanted me to hide away like a frightened little mouse.

GREAT GRANDMOTHER. She would have wanted you to be as brave as a tiger!

IRENE. But I'm not brave. They have told me such stories of thieves and goblins and monsters that I am frightened of every little thing.

GREAT GRANDMOTHER. That is how fear serves us – it always sides with the thing we are afraid of.

IRENE. Then I will try never to be afraid…Tomorrow, when I'm taken for my walk, I'll run to the mountain… Lootie is too slow to catch me…I'll run and run…Into the great wide open…*(yawns)*

GREAT GRANDMOTHER. That's my girl, but you're sleepy now. I have something to give you so you do not wake and think me only a dream. *(takes a ring from her finger)* Here.

IRENE. What a beautiful ring! What is the stone called?

GREAT GRANDMOTHER. It's a fire-opal.

IRENE. Please, am I to keep it?

GREAT GRANDMOTHER. Always.

IRENE. Oh, thank you…*(puts in on her finger)* But what will I tell Lootie when she asks where I got it?

GREAT GRANDMOTHER. You must ask her where you got it.

IRENE. I don't understand.

GREAT GRANDMOTHER. Trust me…Now, you must go back down to your bed. You'll find your way, I promise.

IRENE. I'll go…But how can I find you again?

GREAT GRANDMOTHER. *(resumes spinning)* I ask only that you believe in me.

IRENE. I believe…I haven't even asked what you are spinning…

GREAT GRANDMOTHER. That will wait for another time. Goodnight, little Irene, and remember – as brave as a tiger. *(vanishes)*

IRENE. Yes…A tiger…As brave as a tiger…Running in the great wide open…

*(**IRENE** goes.)*

Scene Three

(Open countryside, in the shadow of the great mountain.)

*(**SLY**, an ugly, sinister goblin-creature moves fleetingly behind the rocks.)*

KRANKL. *(from off)* Come to me, my little spy…

*(Enter **CROWN PRINCE KRANKL**, shielding his eyes against the sun.)*

Come, your prince commands it!

*(**SLY** runs to him, crouches at his feet.)*

Tell me, Sly, have you seen her? Have you found her?

*(**SLY** shakes his head.)*

Their sun blinds me, so you must be my eyes…until it is dark! Look until you find this girl called Irene, and then I'll come and take her away. *(rounds on **AUDIENCE**)* And there's nothing you can do to stop me! Stupid brats! One day I'll be king of you all, and I'll have respect from you then! Oh yes I will!

AUDIENCE. Oh no you won't!

KRANKL. Oh yes I will!

AUDIENCE. Oh no you won't!

KRANKL. By the time I'm finished with you they'll have to scrape you off the floor! *(to **SLY**)* Go now, Sly, and when you find her, run to my cave and the goblins will fly to her as fast as lightning –

*(**SLY** runs off.)*

– and then you will see how cruel I can really be! *(**KRANKL** goes.)*

*(Enter **PRINCESS IRENE**.)*

IRENE. *(shouting off)* Come on, come on! I'm not going fast.

*(Enter **NURSE LOOTIE**, struggling for breath.)*

LOOTIE. Too fast for me…*(leans on her stick)*

IRENE. Then I'll leave you behind…

LOOTIE. Don't leave me here!…You've never run this far before…*(looks up)* How high the mountain is. It's like a great evil giant waiting to fall on us. *(shivers)*

IRENE. *(takes her hand)* It's not evil. The trees by the river are hung all over with drops of rain. They sparkle like jewels in the sun.

LOOTIE. Just like your ring… Never seen such a glow. It's a fiery rose burning on your finger.

IRENE. My ring?… I must ask you, Lootie, where did I get this ring?

LOOTIE. It belonged to your mother. She will have left it to you.

IRENE. My mother's ring…*(kisses it)* I will never lose it.

LOOTIE. It will soon be dark. *(pulls* **IRENE** *after her)* We must not be out a moment longer!

IRENE. *(pulling free)* Don't be frightened, Lootie.

LOOTIE. Don't be ridiculous! I am never frightened!

IRENE. Of course not…Look, Lootie, look! A face, a face!

LOOTIE. *(screaming in fear)* Where, where!

IRENE. There, behind the rocks! And look, Lootie, look! At the foot of that old tree!

*(**LOOTIE** screams.)*

What a funny creature, and it's making faces at you… *(laughs, makes a face)*

LOOTIE. *(seeing her laughter)* Irene, the lies you tell! *(brandishes stick)* I've a good mind to warm your ears…

*(**SLY** appears from the rocks, behind **IRENE**. **LOOTIE** screams and points.)*

A face, a face!

IRENE. You must think I'm stupid…

*(**IRENE** turns to look, but **SLY** has hidden.)*

You can't fool me…

*(turns back to **LOOTIE**)*

*(**SLY** reappears. **LOOTIE**, too terrified to speak, turns **IRENE** round to face **SLY**.)*

IRENE. *(cont.) (seeing* SLY, *shouts out in fear)* Go away, whoever you are! Go away! *(advances on* SLY) I'm not frightened, do you hear! You don't frighten me!

*(*SLY *runs off.)*

Oh, but Lootie, I am frightened.

LOOTIE. Hurry, we must leave here!

IRENE. Yes, this way!

LOOTIE. No, this way! I remember that rock.

IRENE. No, this way! I remember that tree.

LOOTIE. I've forgotten our way home. We're lost, lost!

IRENE. Follow me, I'm sure I'm right.

*(*IRENE *takes* LOOTIE*'s hand, they run, but stop suddenly.)*

Over there – shadows on the rock!

LOOTIE. They're coming out of the ground!

(They rush in another direction, but an urgent whispering comes from all around them.)

IRENE. Voices – all around us.

(They hold each other close.)

They're coming, Lootie, they're coming for us!

*(Enter a Miner-boy (*CURDIE*) with a pick-axe over his shoulder. He sings out in a strong voice.)*

CURDIE. Ring! Dod! Bang!
Hear the hammers' clang!
Hit and turn and bore!
Whizz and puff and roar!
Smash the diamond rocks!
Force the goblins' locks!

LOOTIE. Be quiet! They'll hear you!

*(*CURDIE *sings even louder, to the unseen enemy.)*

CURDIE. Hush! Shush! Scurry!
There you go in a hurry!
Gobble! Gobble! Goblin!
There you go a-wobblin'!

Hobble, hobble, hobblin'!
Cobble! Cobble! Cobblin!
Hob-hob-goblin! – *(shouts defiantly)* Haaaaah!

(He listens, and the whispering has ceased.)

There! That's shown them!

LOOTIE. *(amazed)* They've gone!

IRENE. How did you do that? Are you a magician?

CURDIE. *(laughing)* No…Goblins hate dreams, and what are songs but dreams set to music? They won't touch you as long as I'm with you.

LOOTIE. And who exactly are you?

CURDIE. I'm Peter's son.

IRENE. Who's Peter?

CURDIE. Peter the miner.

LOOTIE. I don't know him.

CURDIE. *(shrugs)* I'm his son though.

LOOTIE. And why should the goblins mind a dirty little miner boy?

CURDIE. It's easy…If you're not afraid of them, they're afraid of you.

IRENE. Who told you that?

CURDIE. I know about goblins because I work under the mountain where they live. But it's a different thing down there. If you get frightened of them, or get a rhyme wrong, then they really give you a doing!

IRENE. What do they do?

CURDIE. Well, first they…

LOOTIE. Don't go frightening the princess!

CURDIE. The princess! *(bows)* I beg your pardon, but I hope they didn't hear you call her princess or they will be sure to remember her. They may be strange and ugly to us but they're as sharp as my knife.

LOOTIE. Hurry, hurry, we must run home!

CURDIE. Never run! That only makes them worse. I'll take you home. Shall I carry the little princess?

LOOTIE. The impertinence!

IRENE. I can walk perfectly well, and besides, I don't even know your name.

CURDIE. I'm Curdie…Curdie Peterson. What's your name?

LOOTIE. *(sternly, to* **CURDIE***)* Your Royal Highness to you!

IRENE. No, Lootie. It's rude to call people silly names. Please, Curdie Peterson, I am Irene.

CURDIE. I'm pleased to meet you, Irene. Come on, I'll take you home.

IRENE. You're very kind, but I can manage by myself.

*(***LOOTIE*** throws up her arms in frustration.)*

CURDIE. If you're sure.

IRENE. I'm quite sure. *(offers her hand)* Thank-you for all your help.

CURDIE. *(shaking her hand.)* Goodbye, Irene.

IRENE. Goodbye, Curdie Peterson.

(He goes.)

LOOTIE. Foolish girl! How will we find our way now?

IRENE. Where's your pride, Lootie? I know the way, so follow me… *(with great certainty)* He has chased away the goblins so there is nothing to be afraid of, absolutely nothing…

*(***KRANKL*** appears right in front of her, and she screams in fright.)*

KRANKL. Good evening, Your Royal Highness.

IRENE. *(shaking with fear)* Who…who are you?

KRANKL. It is only right that you are a princess since I am Crown Prince Krankl of The Great Goblin Race. *(bows low)* At your service!

IRENE. G-good evening, Prince Krankl, and goodbye…
*(***IRENE*** runs with **LOOTIE***.)*

*(***KRANKL*** whistles and **KING COB** appears and blocks their way. They try another route, but **SLY** appears, hissing like a snake.)*

KRANKL. Have a care. He has the bite of a snake!

*(***IRENE*** walks right up to **KRANKL***.)*

IRENE. Get out of my way!

KRANKL. *(amazed)* What did you say?

IRENE. You heard! You're standing where I want to walk. We're going home now… *(walks)*

KRANKL. *(blocking her way)* What use is courage in an ugly world? *(produces black sack)* No, princess, I will put you in my black sack and carry you down to my kingdom beneath the mountain. Seize her!

*(**KING COB** seizes her, and they make to carry her off. **NURSE LOOTIE** shouts in alarm. **CURDIE** flies into their midst swinging his pick-axe.)*

CURDIE. One, two – hit and hew!

Three, four – blast and bore!

*(The goblins hold their ears and scream in pain. **KING COB** recovers and charges at **CURDIE**, who stamps on his foot. **KING COB** flees. **SLY** approaches, hissing evilly, but **CURDIE** aims a blow at him and he runs off into the darkness. **KRANKL** draws his sword and launches a vicious attack. **CURDIE** holds him off with his pick-axe, singing all the time.)*

Gobble! Gobble! Goblin!

There you go a-wobblin'!

Hobble, hobble, hobblin'!

Cobble! Cobble! Cobblin!

Hob-hob-goblin! – Haaaaaah!

*(He stamps on **KRANKL**'s foot and **KRANKL** retreats, defeated.)*

KRANKL. Krankl will not forget this! He will have your blood! He will have your bones! *(**KRANKL** flees.)*

CURDIE. *(breathing hard)* Always go for their feet! Their heads and bodies are as hard as rock but their feet have no toes and they are soft as earth. Stamp on their feet! Remember now!

IRENE. I won't forget…Are you hurt, Curdie Peterson?

CURDIE. I'm not hurt.

LOOTIE. *(in despair)* Someone, please – take me home to my bed!

IRENE. *(to* **CURDIE***)* I was too stupid to ask before – Will you take me home?

CURDIE. Yes, easy.

LOOTIE. I'll give you half-a-crown for your trouble.

IRENE. And I promise to give you a kiss.

LOOTIE. Mercy me!

CURDIE. Very well, Princess Irene... *(Takes her hands and spins her round and round.)* And you too, old nanny... *(Spins* **LOOTIE** *round and round.)* There's the palace there, see, just behind a rock. You've been running in circles and you've been home all the time. You wouldn't have got lost if you hadn't got frightened.

IRENE. You sound very like my Great Old Grandmother.

LOOTIE. *(muttering)* Great Old Nothing... Girl's not right in the head.

IRENE. Won't you come into the palace?

CURDIE. With all those grand people?... No, I must go to work.

IRENE. Under the mountain...*(shudders)* I could never go there.

CURDIE. I'm used to it. But one day... One day I'll cross the great mountain and walk down into the far countries of the world.

IRENE. The far countries of the world...

LOOTIE. Fiddlesticks! No-one has ever crossed the great mountain!

IRENE. No-one? Not ever?

CURDIE. Not ever.

IRENE. Then perhaps you will be the first.

CURDIE. Perhaps I will.

LOOTIE. In your dreams! This is the country where you live and where you die, and there's an end to it!

IRENE. Be careful, Lootie, or one day you'll turn into a goblin.

LOOTIE. *(offers coin to* **CURDIE***)* Here's your money, boy… Off with you, now!

CURDIE. Keep your money!

IRENE. But I will give you a kiss.

LOOTIE. You'll do no such thing!

IRENE. But I promised!

LOOTIE. A princess kissing a miner-boy! Over my dead body! *(to* **CURDIE***, brandishing her stick)* On your way, boy! Shoo, shoo!

CURDIE. Never mind, Princess Irene. You don't have to kiss me tonight, but perhaps I'll come another time. Good-night, Irene. *(***CURDIE** *goes.)*

IRENE. Goodnight, Curdie Peterson…*(rounds on* **LOOTIE***, furious.)* Lootie, you've made me break my promise!

LOOTIE. And as for you – get up those stairs to your bed before I break this stick over your head!

IRENE. There's someone I must talk to…*(runs off)*

LOOTIE. Head full of nonsense…Kissing miner-boys, and her royalty too! Not that I'm old-fashioned, not a bit of it! I'm all for change, so I am, just as long as everything stays the same…

*(***LOOTIE***, exits, muttering under her breath, shaking her head.)*

Scene Four

(The attic rooms high up in the palace. Enter **IRENE**, *unsure of her way.)*

IRENE. Show yourself – please! I've looked in every room and I can't find you anywhere. Please, Great Grandmother! *(looks around hopefully)* Nothing, that's all you were, nothing but a stupid dream!…*(touches her ring)* My mother's ring…*(remembers)* So you do not wake and think me a dream…I'm sure that's what she said. *(closes her eyes)* I do believe…I believe that when I open my eyes I will see you again. *(The humming sound commences.)* What a lovely sound!

(The **GREAT GRANDMOTHER** *is revealed, spinning at her wheel.)*

Please be there! *(opens her eyes)* I've found you!

GREAT GRANDMOTHER. You would have found me a lot sooner if you hadn't thought me a dream.

IRENE. Don't be angry.

GREAT GRANDMOTHER. I'm not angry. Come here, child.

*(***IRENE** *runs to her, and they embrace.)*

IRENE. I ran to the mountain and the goblins came for me… And then he came to save me…Curdie Peterson…If I ever see him again I will bring him to meet you.

GREAT GRANDMOTHER. I would thank him for his courage.

IRENE. He's like you – he's not afraid of anything.

GREAT GRANDMOTHER. But I was afraid today, Irene – for you. They nearly took you away, and that is why I must give you something to keep you safe.

IRENE. What is it?

GREAT GRANDMOTHER. *(resumes spinning)* Can you tell me what I'm spinning?

IRENE. *(shaking her head)* I can't see anything.

GREAT GRANDMOTHER. It's a magic thread.

IRENE. Magic!

GREAT GRANDMOTHER. Yes, and I am spinning it for you.

IRENE. But it's invisible.

GREAT GRANDMOTHER. That's because it is made from light itself, from the light of my very own moon… *(stops spinning)* It's finished now. Here, Irene, my gift to you – a ball of magic thread.

IRENE. Thank-you…But if it is magic what am I to do with it?

GREAT GRANDMOTHER. Give me your ring…There…I have tied one end of the thread to your ring, and the other end I will keep with me. *(**GREAT GRANDMOTHER** puts the ring back on **IRENE***'s finger.)* If you're ever frightened or in danger you must follow the thread wherever it leads.

IRENE. But I can't see it.

GREAT GRANDFATHER. It is too fine to be seen…You must feel your way, like this, with your ringfinger. Try it.

IRENE. I can feel it! *(**IRENE** follows it, and it leads her back to her **GREAT GRANDMOTHER**.)* It will always lead me to you.

GREAT GRANDMOTHER. Always, but first it may take you to places you don't want to go, yet you must always trust the magic of the thread! Promise me, now.

IRENE. I promise.

GREAT GRANDMOTHER. Of one thing you may be sure – while you hold the thread, I hold it too.

IRENE. You make me strong… *(yawns)*

GREAT GRANDMOTHER. Go down to your bed.

IRENE. Can't I stay the night with you?

GREAT GRANDMOTHER. Your nurse will be worried. *(Kisses her.)* Go down to her.

IRENE. Thank-you for your present…It's wonderful…Now I can be as brave as Curdie Peterson…I hope I see him again…

GREAT GRANDMOTHER. Trust the thread.

IRENE. I will…Goodnight, Great Grandmother…*(**IRENE** goes.)*

GREAT GRANDMOTHER. Goodnight, Irene. Who knows how magic works its wonder? The thread may lead her to many dark and dangerous places on her way back to me. *(to* **AUDIENCE***)* If you see her, will you help her for me?

AUDIENCE. Yes,

GREAT GRANDMOTHER. Even though it's very dangerous?

AUDIENCE. Yes.

GREAT GRANDMOTHER. Thank-you. You're very brave. *(***GREAT GRANDMOTHER** *vanishes.)*

Scene Five

(The mines, deep under the great mountain. The sound of distant hammering.)

(Enter CURDIE *and his* FATHER, *with lamps.)*

CURDIE. This way, Father! They're here, just through the rock!

FATHER. No, son, the goblins never work this part of the mountain.

CURDIE. Use your ears! *(listens to the ground)*

FATHER. *(listens)* You're right…I'd know their sound anywhere – goblin hammers!

CURDIE. What can they be up to?

FATHER. Pure badness, what else?

CURDIE. They've never gone this far down before. *(touches the rock)* Even the rock is hot!

FATHER. The heart of the earth is made up of melting hot metals and stones – a huge power of buried sunlight that heats and cracks the rock until it sparkles with gold and silver…

CURDIE. Copper and tin…

FATHER. Mercury, coal and iron…

CURDIE. Diamonds, rubies and emeralds…

FATHER. Only a miner knows the secrets of a mountain for it's his business to bring to light hidden things.

CURDIE. If only we could bring to light the goblins' plan.

(Voices are heard.)

FATHER. Quiet! Someone's coming!

CURDIE. Hide, Father!

FATHER. I'm not frightened of any goblin!

CURDIE. We'll learn nothing if they see us… Hide and listen! *(They hide.)*

(Enter QUEEN MAM *and* PRINCE KRANKL, *laughing.)*

QUEEN MAM. What a plan! It couldn't be better!

KRANKL. It really makes me laugh to think of the mess we'll make of them all up there!

QUEEN MAM. We'll teach them a lesson they'll never forget!

KRANKL. We'll hurt them all right! I can't stop laughing!

QUEEN MAM. Neither can I!

(Exeunt **KRANKL** *and* **MAM,** *laughing evilly.* **CURDIE** *and his* **FATHER** *come out of hiding.)*

FATHER. The Queen and The Prince!

CURDIE. I must follow them and find out their evil plan.

FATHER. *(making to go)* Hurry, then.

CURDIE. No, Father, I'll go myself.

FATHER. You'll lose your way in the endless caverns.

CURDIE. *(tying string to his pickaxe)* My pick will be my anchor. This string will guide me back.

FATHER. Clever boy.

CURDIE. Tell mother I'll be home by morning.

FATHER. She knows you're quick and strong…but remember your rhymes…

CURDIE. I'll remember…Goodbye, Father. *(goes, trailing string)*

FATHER. *(calling after him)* And don't forget their soft feet… He won't forget. He's a match for any goblin in the mountain. There's nothing they can do to hurt him. *(*FATHER *goes.)*

(Enter **SLY,** *the goblin spy. He goes to* **CURDIE***'s pickaxe, hissing with pleasure. He lifts up the pick-axe and exits in pursuit of* **CURDIE,** *carrying the pick-axe and following the string.)*

(Deeper under the great mountain. Enter **CURDIE,** *cautiously, paying out his string.)*

CURDIE. They can't be far. I'm sure I've caught up with them…

*(*CURDIE *hears the sound of* QUEEN MAM *groaning in discomfort.)*

They're here! Now we'll find out their plan. *(He hides.)*

(Enter QUEEN MAM. *She puts down a tray of glasses full of a vile-looking liquid.)*

QUEEN MAM. *(checks the coast is clear)* Now's your chance, Queenie! There's no-one here. My shoes are killing me! I'm in agony! *(takes shoe off and rubs her toes)* Suffer it, girl – you have to wear shoes of stone to hide your horrible toes.

You could never be Queen of the goblins if they knew you had toes on your feet. If I had the courage I'd chop them off with the royal axe! *(Voices are heard.)* They're coming! Quickly – they must never see my toes! Hide the toes! On with the shoe, on with the shoe! *(puts shoe on)*

*(Enter **PRINCE KRANKL** and **KING COB** in high spirits.)*

KING COB. The same tunnel for two plans – perfect, my boy!

QUEEN MAM. It's a perfect plan because it was thought up by our son who is perfect in every way.

*(**QUEEN MAM** kisses **KRANKL**.)*

KRANKL. Yes, I know.

QUEEN MAM. The pet.

KING COB. Nothing can stop us. Day and night a huge army of goblins are digging the tunnel. Soon it will be finished and then, oh yes, then!

QUEEN MAM. Let's drink a toast to the terror we will bring. *(hands round drinks)*

KING COB. Worm wine – my favourite!

KRANKL. *(offering a toast)* Death to dreams.

QUEEN MAM, **KING COB.** *(in unison)* Death to dreams!

*(They drink, gargle, shake their heads and swallow. The **QUEEN** stamps her massive rock-clad feet.)*

QUEEN MAM. Deelumcious!

KING COB. And just think if the First Plan fails then all we have to do is use the same tunnel for the Second Plan…

KRANKL. When we will burst open the walls of the great underground lake!…But the First Plan will not fail! I will have the sun-girl! I must! I must!

QUEEN MAM. We know you are only thinking of your duty.

KRANKL. Of course I am, mother, but it will be fun to make her cry.

KING COB. Great fun!

KRANKL. There is one other I would dearly love to hurt – a miner-boy who fought with me, a maker of rhymes… If I could get my hands on him, I would show no mercy!

QUEEN MAM. I'll drink to that. *(offers toast)* No mercy!

KRANKL, KING COB. *(in unison)* No mercy!

> *(They drink, gargle, shake their heads and swallow. The* **QUEEN** *stamps her feet, and, by accident stamps on* **CURDIE**'s *hand. He shouts in pain and scrambles to his feet.)*

KING COB. A spy!

KRANKL. It's him! It's the miner-boy!

CURDIE. Stay back!

QUEEN MAM. Get him!

KING COB. You get him!

QUEEN MAM. You get him first!

KRANKL. We'll get him together. *(They move towards* **CURDIE**.*)* You're claimed, miner-boy!

CURDIE. Once there was a goblin

> Living in a hole!
> Busy he was cobblin'
> A shoe without a sole!

> *(The* **GOBLINS** *hold their ears in pain, but continue their advance.)*

> What's the good o' that, sir,
> Working in your hole?
> You never can have soles, sir,
> For a goblin has no soul!

> *(The goblins cease their advance.)*

QUEEN MAM. *(screaming)* Stop that disgusting noise!

CURDIE. I'll stop, but only if you leave me alone...Stay back, and I'll be on my way.

KRANKL. You'll never find your way out!

CURDIE. That's what you think! *(holds up string)* I'm not stupid, I know my way. So goodnight your Royal Highnesses, and good riddance! *(turns to go)*

> *(Enter* **SLY**, *hissing with triumph, holding* **CURDIE**'s *pick-axe.)*

No!

KRANKL. Ha! You're in trouble now, boy! You're for the chop!

CURDIE. I'd stay back if I was you!

QUEEN MAM. An impossible if!

CURDIE. I'm warning you!

KING COB. Don't make me laugh!

CURDIE. All right – I won't!

(He snatches his pick from **SLY** *and clobbers* **KING COB**.*)*

Come on, then! Come on! Who's next?

(He swings at **SLY**, *who flees in terror.* **KING COB**, *recovered,* **KRANKL** *and* **QUEEN MAM** *surround* **CURDIE** *and begin to close in.)*

Gobble! Gobble! Goblin!
There you go a-wobblin'!

*(***CURDIE** *stamps on* **KING COB***'s foot.)*

Hobble, hobble, hobblin'!
Cobble! Cobble! Cobblin'!

*(***CURDIE** *stamps on* **KRANKL***'s foot.)*

Hob-hob-goblin! – Haaaaaaah!

(He stamps on **QUEEN MAM***'s foot, but it has no effect whatsoever.)*

QUEEN MAM. *(with an evil grin)* You've forgotten, haven't you, dear – you've forgotten all about my little shoesies!

(She stamps on **CURDIE***'s foot who shouts in pain, and hops on one foot.)*

Does it hurt? Poor diddums.

(She stamps on his other foot, and **CURDIE** *drops his pick-axe.)*

Seize him!

*(***KING COB** *grabs hold of him.* **KRANKL** *takes up the pick-axe and threatens* **CURDIE** *with it.)*

KRANKL. One more rhyme out of you and I'll break your head!

CURDIE. I'm not scared of you!

QUEEN MAM. Well you should be, you horrible little human! Squash him, squash him so he can't escape!

(They throw **CURDIE** *to the ground.* **QUEEN MAM** *holds him down with one of her rock-shod feet while* **KRANKL** *and* **KING COB** *pile heavy boulders and slabs of rock on top of him.)*

Thay's the way, boys! Bury him under a mountain of rock! Pile them on, pile them on!

CURDIE. Stop it! That hurts!

KRANKL. It's meant to hurt!

KING COB. Now that we have him, what will we do with him?

KRANKL. Let mother decide. It was she who caught him with her wonderful shoes.

QUEEN MAM. Sweet boy! Now, I must think up something really cruel! *(***QUEEN MAM** *thinks.)*

KRANKL. Come on, mummy, you can do it!

QUEEN MAM. We could always starve him to death, but that would be a terrible waste.

KING COB. You're not going to eat him!

QUEEN MAM. *(grimaces)* I wouldn't lower myself, but, listen here, boys – might not our pets find him a very tasty dish?

KRANKL. Genius! Did you hear, miner-boy? In the morning I'm going to feed you to Fannon, the fiercest of my pets!

QUEEN MAM. *(to* **CURDIE.***)* So night-night, then, dearie. Sweet dreams. *(laughs)*

CURDIE. Go to bed,

Goblin, do.

Help the queen

Take off her shoe!

(The goblins clutch their heads in agony.)

If you do

It will disclose

A perfect set

Of sprouting toes!

QUEEN MAM. *(screaming in pain and rage)* Toes, toes! The insolence! The very idea! Goblins never have toes! Only horrible humans have toes!…My head hurts!

KING COB. That reminds me, dear wife – in all the years we've been married, I have never seen your feet.

QUEEN MAM. What!!!!

KING COB. I thought perhaps you might take your shoes off in bed tonight…They dig in so.

KRANKL. Are you suggesting my mother has toes?

KING COB. I'm sorry I ever spoke.

QUEEN MAM. Never been so insulted! *(cuffs **KING COB**)*

KING COB. I meant no offence, Great Queen.

QUEEN MAM. To bed! As long as I'm Queen here I'll sleep with my shoes on! It is my royal privilege! Everyone – to bed! *(drags **KING COB**)* And as for you! You'd better be good or I'll…And then I'll…

KING COB. Oh, no, no…*(She drags him off.)*

KRANKL. I've changed my mind, miner-boy. I'm not going to feed you to Fannon in the morning – I'm going to feed you to him now! I'll be back for you!

*(**KRANKL** exits, laughing.)*

CURDIE. *(struggles in vain against the rocks)* She tricked me with her shoes! How could I be so stupid? *(shouts out loud)* But don't think I'll give up because I won't! I'll think up a rhyme so strong it'll blow your heads off!… I can't think of anything! *(a distant roar)* They're coming for me…

VOICE. *(from off)* Is there anyone there?

CURDIE. Here they come! *(closes his eyes)*

*(Enter **PRINCESS IRENE**, barefoot, in her nightdress. Her eyes are closed as she follows her invisible thread.)*

IRENE. I thought I heard a voice I knew.

CURDIE. *(opening his eyes)* Princess Irene!

IRENE. *(opening her eyes.)* It is you! Curdie Peterson!

CURDIE. Sssh! They'll hear you!

IRENE. You were shouting loud.

CURDIE. They know I'm here, they don't know you are. How did you find me?

IRENE. I dreamed I was all alone in the world and when I woke up I was very frightened – so I followed my grandmother's magic thread. Instead of leading me up to her room, it led me outside and down under the mountain. *(follows thread)* It has led me to you… *(IRENE kneels by CURDIE.)*

CURDIE. I don't understand any of that.

IRENE. *(heaving at a rock)* I know, but that's no reason why I shouldn't say it…It's too heavy, I can't move it.

CURDIE. My pick-axe, quickly!

(a blood-curling roar, nearer now)

IRENE. *(brings the pick)* What's that sound?

CURDIE. Don't ask!

(They lever off the heavy slabs with the pick-axe.)

KRANKL. *(from off)* We're coming, miner-boy! We're coming for you!

IRENE. *(moving the last stone)* There – you're free!

CURDIE. *(leaping to his feet)* This way!

IRENE. No, this way.

CURDIE. What!!!

IRENE. I must follow my magic thread.

CURDIE. *(scornfully)* Magic thread!

(another roar)

KRANKL. *(off)* Do you hear, miner-boy! Fannon is famished!

IRENE. Trust me…*(holds out her hand)*

(CURDIE takes her hand, and they run off.)

(Enter KRANKL with FANNON, a fierce and handsome young dragon, straining against his leash.)

KRANKL. Behold my dragon! He is too young to breathe fire, but his teeth are like razors! He will crunch your bones! *(slips the leash)* On you go, boy – get torn in! *(FANNON remains still.)* What are you waiting for?…

(looks round) He's gone…Impossible! *(shouts out)* Wake up, goblins! The prisoner has escaped! Mother, father! Chase him, Fannon! After him, my pet!

(**FANNON** *runs off.*)

The blood is up! The hunt is on!

(**KRANKL** *runs off.*)

(Enter **IRENE** *and* **CURDIE**. **IRENE** *follows the thread.)*

IRENE. We'll be out soon.

CURDIE. How do you know?

IRENE. Because my grandmother is taking care of us. *(takes his hand)* There…Feel the thread.

CURDIE. I can't feel anything…*(pulls his hand away)* Stupid!

IRENE. If you can't feel it, you shouldn't call it stupid!

(Voices are heard.)

CURDIE. They're right behind us! Quickly – hide! *(pulls* **IRENE** *into hiding)*

(Enter **KING COB** *and* **QUEEN MAM**, *at a run.)*

QUEEN MAM. He's getting away! After him!

KING COB. *(stopping)* I am after him! *(They collide.)*

QUEEN MAM. Fool! Move yourself! *(kicks him)*

KING COB. I'm moving, I'm moving! *(They run off.)*

IRENE. *(coming out of hiding)* They've gone.

CURDIE. No. Irene – get back! *(pulls* **IRENE** *back into hiding)*

(Enter **SLY**, *searching, hissing malevolently. He crosses and exits.* **CURDIE** *and* **IRENE** *come out of hiding.)*

I think we're safe now.

(A low, rumbling roar and **FANNON** *enters.)*

It's a dragon! Run, Princess!

IRENE. His wing, look, it's wounded.

CURDIE. He's the fiercest of all their pets! You go on, Princess Irene – go on! *(faces* **FANNON**, *brandishing his pick)* Come on, then, Fannon! *(The Dragon roars fiercely.)* If you want to eat me, you'll have to fight me first!

IRENE. *(goes right up to* **FANNON***)* Sssh, now, quiet…

CURDIE. *(astonished)* What are you doing?

IRENE. You're a good dragon, aren't you? *(***FANNON***, amazed, roars murderously.)* Yes, you are.

CURDIE. He'll tear you to pieces!

IRENE. Stop that noise now, and let me look at your wing… *(examines wing)* There – that's the trouble…*(pulls out spike)*

CURDIE. A goblin spike! No wonder he's so bad-tempered.

IRENE. *(stroking* **FANNON***)* That's better now, isn't it? *(***FANNON*** *licks her face.)* Stop licking!

CURDIE. His wings are only new-grown. He's no older than five or six.

IRENE. Six years in this terrible darkness! You poor beast!

(angry shouts from offstage)

CURDIE. Hurry – The Prince!

IRENE. *(to* **FANNON***)* Won't you come with us? *(***FANNON*** *makes no move.)*

CURDIE. This is his home, princess.

IRENE. Goodbye, Fannon – I won't forget you.

*(***IRENE*** *takes* **CURDIE***'s hand and goes, following her thread.)*

(Enter **CROWN PRINCE KRANKL.***)*

KRANKL. Hurry, Fannon! He's bound to get lost and we'll track him down! *(to* **AUDIENCE***)* Oh yes, we'll catch him, and you'll help us. *(points the right way)* He went that way, didn't he?

AUDIENCE. No!

KRANKL. *(points the wrong way)* Then he went that way, didn't he?

AUDIENCE. Yes!

KRANKL. I don't trust you! Fannon will lead me to him! On you go, boy! *(***FANNON*** *runs off in entirely the wrong direction.)* I'll show you, brats! I'm Prince of the mountain! After him! After him!

*(***KRANKL*** *exits, following* **FANNON***.)*

Scene Six

(The open mountainside. The moon and stars shine brightly.)

(Enter **IRENE** *and* **CURDIE**, *at a run.)*

CURDIE. We're free, Irene, free!

IRENE. We must thank my great old grandmother…

CURDIE. But where have you brought us out to? I know the mountain, but not this cliff or that peak or that river…

IRENE. My thread will lead us home.

CURDIE. Look, Irene! Over there! A path leads up the mountainside…Up and up and up! All my life I've dreamed of finding this secret place! If we followed the path it would lead us over the great mountain…

IRENE. And down into the far countries of the world.

CURDIE. Come with me, Irene! *(takes her hand)* Come with me now!

IRENE. And leave them all behind…That would be lovely… But I must follow my thread… *(**IRENE** lets go of his hand.)*

CURDIE. And I must be home by morning or my father will go looking for me in the mines.

IRENE. Never mind, Curdie Peterson. First you must come with me to the palace.

CURDIE. A palace is no place for a miner-boy.

IRENE. There is someone I want you to meet.

CURDIE. If you wish it.

IRENE. I wish it. This way – follow me.

*(**IRENE** goes.)*

CURDIE. *(to the mountain.)* One day, great mountain…one day!

*(**CURDIE** goes after her.)*

Scene Seven

(The palace. Enter **NURSE LOOTIE,** *in high dudgeon.)*

LOOTIE. Princess Irene! Where are you? Up all night looking for her…The stupid, selfish little girl! Wait till I get my hands on her!

*(***LOOTIE*** exits.)*

(Enter **IRENE** *and* **CURDIE***.)*

CURDIE. And as for The Queen – She has toes on her feet.

IRENE. Like we do?

CURDIE. Yes, and that's why she wears shoes – to hide her toes…

(Enter **LOOTIE***.)*

LOOTIE. *(thunderous)* So there you are! Where have you been, girl!

IRENE. I've…

LOOTIE. And what's he doing here?

IRENE. He's…

LOOTIE. Well, he's not welcome! I suppose you've been hiding again.

IRENE. I have not been hiding!

LOOTIE. Then where have you been?

IRENE. If you would listen I'll tell you!

LOOTIE. Very well, I'm listening, but it had better be the truth!

IRENE. I followed my magic thread. It led me deep down under the mountain where I found my friend Curdie Peterson, and now I'm taking him up to meet my great old Grandmother who lives in the attic.

LOOTIE. Oh yes, of course…Telling silly lies! You must think I'm stupid!

IRENE. Yes, I suppose I do…

LOOTIE. *(murderous)* What did you say?

CURDIE. She saved me from the goblins – that is true!

LOOTIE. No-one asked you!

IRENE. I tell the truth and you say don't tell lies! Maybe, if I tell lies, you might believe me!

LOOTIE. A miner-boy…It's no way for a princess to behave!

IRENE. *(exploding with rage and frustration)* How do you think a princess should behave? Leave me immediately! I am a princess and you a servant so you must do as you are told! Is that better behaviour for a princess?

LOOTIE. *(to **CURDIE**)* You'll have put her up to this!

IRENE. Leave my sight, I mean it! *(**IRENE** snatches **LOOTIE**'s stick from her, prods her with it.)* Or I will tell my father I want another nurse, a nurse who knows how to behave! *(**LOOTIE** starts to protest.)* Don't interrupt! Now go, and I don't want to see you again until I call for you! Is that understood? Well, is it?

LOOTIE. *(after a pause)* Yes, Your Highness.

IRENE. *(hands her back her stick)* Goodnight, then, Lootie.

LOOTIE. Goodnight, Your Highness.

> *(**LOOTIE** curtsies and exits.)*

IRENE. *(leaps with triumph)* Yes! Yes! Yes!…I'm sorry, Curdie Peterson, she makes me angry…

CURDIE. I should never have come here.

IRENE. Don't let her hurt you…This way, come on…*(takes his hands, spins him around)* Up the narrow stair…Up and up and up…Right to the very top of the palace… Don't be frightened…She's here, I know she is…

> *(Enter **GREAT GRANDMOTHER**.)*

GREAT GRANDMOTHER. Welcome, Irene. I've been waiting for you.

IRENE. *(runs to her)* I've brought Curdie Peterson to see you.

GREAT GRANDMOTHER. I'm glad to meet him. He is good and brave.

IRENE. Yes, he is, even if he didn't believe me about you… But he will now. Well, Curdie, won't you say hullo to my Great Old Grandmother?

> *(**CURDIE** stares, utterly bewildered.)*

Don't be shy! Say something.

CURDIE. I don't see any Grandmother.

IRENE. Of course you do! She's here, right beside me.

CURDIE. There's something…*(shivers)* But it's only a feeling…There's nothing there!

IRENE. Then what do you see?

CURDIE. *(shrugs)* I see a room.

IRENE. Yes, the most beautiful room in all the world!

CURDIE. A big, bare attic room…There's a moonbeam coming through a hole in the roof and shining on your head…That's all…I think you should stop it, princess.

IRENE. *(to* **GREAT GRANDMOTHER***)* I don't understand.

GREAT GRANDMOTHER. You must give him time.

IRENE. *(to* **CURDIE***)* But don't you hear my Grandmother talking to me?

CURDIE. I hear the wind blowing in the chimneys…You rescued me from the goblins, and I thank you for that, but you didn't have to bring me all the way up here just to make me look a fool! Goodbye…

IRENE. No, Curdie…

CURDIE. I may only be a miner-boy, but I'm not stupid!

GREAT GRANDMOTHER. Let him go, Irene.

IRENE. But he's only just got here!

CURDIE. Stop it! There's nothing here! Nothing!

IRENE. My Grandmother says you may go…Turn to the right when you reach the bottom of all the stairs.

CURDIE. Goodbye, Princess Irene!

IRENE. Don't go…

(He goes.)

Gone…I was sure he could see everything.

GREAT GRANDMOTHER. His eyes are as dark as the mines where he works.

IRENE. Yes, but they shine as bright as the crystals in the rock…He can't be blind like Lootie is blind.

GREAT GRANDMOTHER. He'll learn to see when his time comes.

IRENE. I've made him angry and now he'll never like me again.

GREAT GRANDMOTHER. He likes you well enough, have no fear of that…Come with me…Now that you have sent your nurse away, you can stay as long as you wish.

IRENE. If only I knew Curdie was safe.

GREAT GRANDMOTHER. He is already running through the gardens, and soon he will be home with his mother and father. Come…I have lit a fire.

IRENE. That sounds lovely…

GREAT GRANDMOTHER. We'll sit by the bright flames… We'll sing songs and tell stories until the morning comes…And then you'll sleep…You'll sleep…

(**GREAT GRANDMOTHER** *exits with* **IRENE**.)

Scene Eight

*(**CURDIE'S FATHER***'s cottage. Enter **CURDIE** with his* **FATHER** *and* **MOTHER**.*)*

CURDIE. Please – leave me alone!

MOTHER. You must go to your bed and sleep the day away.

CURDIE. I'm not tired!

MOTHER. Then you must eat.

CURDIE. I'm not hungry, mother, I've told you!

FATHER. Mind your manners!

CURDIE. I'm sorry…I'm angry at being so careless and having to be rescued by a silly little liar!

MOTHER. You do not speak of the princess as I would like to hear you.

FATHER. She saved your life at the risk of her own.

CURDIE. Yes, she saved me, but she took me into the palace and played tricks on me…Made me look a fool! All that nonsense about her great old Grandmother, when I could see there was no-one there at all!

MOTHER. She spoke as if she saw her herself, didn't she?

CURDIE. Yes, as if she could see her as clearly as I see you now.

MOTHER. Perhaps some people can see what others can't.

CURDIE. I can't believe that!

MOTHER. Answer me this – how can a girl who knows nothing about the mountain, not even that you were a prisoner inside it, come all that way to find you, and then lead you out again?

CURDIE. I have no answer.

MOTHER. Then you have no right to call her a liar.

FATHER. It is a hard life working in the mines, and I would be sorry if working in the dark had made you blind to the wonder of the world.

CURDIE. I would be sorry too…She is proud and strong…I think in my heart I always believed her.

MOTHER. Then you should have told her so! She's a good and brave girl, and that's more than being a princess!

CURDIE. Now I am ashamed.

FATHER. You did what you did, and next time you'll do better…Tell me, what did you hear of the goblins' plan?

CURDIE. Nothing I could understand. They talked of a tunnel and two plans. In the first The Prince spoke of stealing a sun-girl and the fun he would have hurting her…And if that plan failed they would carry out the second plan and burst open the underground lake…

MOTHER. A sun-girl? They are too proud to steal any but a princess, be sure of it!

CURDIE. Irene! But they could never get past the palace guards.

FATHER. A tunnel?…Think where we heard them digging…

CURDIE. That's it! Their tunnel will bring them out right under the palace!

MOTHER. They will creep silently up from the cellars and steal her away, the devils!

FATHER. And if they fail, they will burst open the lake!

CURDIE. And everyone in our mine and in the palace – they will all be drowned!

MOTHER. We must warn the other miners at once!

FATHER. The goblins will attack the palace first! *(to* **CURDIE***)* You must run to tell them!

CURDIE. They'll never believe a miner-boy.

MOTHER. You're as brave and clever as anyone born in a palace! Never forget it!

CURDIE. I'll make them believe me!

FATHER. Good boy! *(to* **MOTHER***)* Hurry – to the mine!

(**FATHER** *goes with* **MOTHER***.)*

CURDIE. Her eyes…Her eyes are like two pieces of night sky each with a star dissolved in the blue. I won't let them take her! *(brandishes pick-axe)* I'll break the head of anyone who tries!

(**CURDIE** *runs off.)*

Scene Nine

(The palace gardens. Night. The faint sounds of subterranean digging. Enter KING-PAPA.*)*

KING-PAPA. *(shouting out)* To arms! To arms! To the gates and walls! The goblins are up! The goblins are out! Their army gathers on the mountain! Behind every rock and tree there hides a goblin or his creature! Light the fires! Prepare for battle! Death to all intruders!

(Enter CURDIE, *followed by* THE CAPTAIN OF THE GUARD.*)*

CURDIE. Please, your majesty, I must speak with you…

CAPTAIN. *(furious)* I've already warned you!

KING-PAPA. Who is this boy?

CURDIE. I work in your mines…

CAPTAIN. Don't listen, your majesty…All day he has told tales of tunnels and secret plans – tales only fit for children!

CURDIE. It's the truth, believe me!

KING-PAPA. Send him away! I must hurry and find my daughter.

CURDIE. Your majesty…

KING-PAPA. Away, I tell you! *(shouts off)* To arms! To arms! Death to all intruders!

*(*KING-PAPA *goes.)*

CAPTAIN. You heard! Get back to where you came from!

*(*CAPTAIN *goes to leave.)*

CURDIE. *(taking him by the arm)* Please listen, not to me, but to the ground! They put their army on the mountain to trick you. Their real attack will come from under the palace! *(puts his ear to the ground)* Hear their picks and hammers!

CAPTAIN. I can't hear anything!

CURDIE. Listen to the ground! You've got to!

CAPTAIN. *(Puts ear to ground. The sounds of digging cease.)* I hear nothing!

CURDIE. Stopped! They've broken through into the cellars! They're on their way up!

CAPTAIN. Enough of your lies, boy! *(draws sword)* Go home, or it'll be the end of you! I won't tell you again! *(calls out)* To the walls! Everyone – to the walls! *(runs off)*

CURDIE. They will steal her away!…No-one will listen to me! But they've got to listen! *(shouts out at the top of his voice)* The enemy is inside the palace! Hear me! They are climbing up from the cellars! To the palace – if you want to save the princess! Hear me!

(SLY appears behind him, bites him on the neck like a snake.)

Poisoned!…*(sees SLY)* So I can shout no more…

(SLY hisses with triumph, and runs off.)

You won't keep me quiet! *(shouts)* To the palace! They are on the stairs!

(Enter CAPTAIN OF THE GUARDS.)

CAPTAIN. Hold your tongue, boy!

CURDIE. To the palace!…

CAPTAIN. You've had your telling! *(runs him through)*

CURDIE. You must save her…You must…Look – she is coming…The princess is coming! *(He falls down onto his knees, holding his wound.)*

(Enter PRINCESS IRENE, hurried along by KING-PAPA and NURSE LOOTIE.)

KING-PAPA. Quickly – inside to your room!

LOOTIE. This way, hurry!

CURDIE. *(scarcely more than a whisper.)* Princess Irene…

IRENE. *(not seeing him)* Who calls my name?

CAPTAIN. No-one fit to be seen, your highness.

LOOTIE. *(seeing CURDIE)* Only a dirty little beggar-boy…*(to IRENE)* On your way now!

KING-PAPA. Do as you're told!

(IRENE runs off to the palace.)

She will be safe in the palace.

LOOTIE. I will see that she is, your majesty.

KING-PAPA. *(to the* **CAPTAIN.***)* Quickly – to the gates! *(goes with* **CAPTAIN.***)*

LOOTIE. *(standing over* **CURDIE***)* If it isn't the insolent little miner-boy! Well, you've got what you deserve, if you want my opinion! Kissing a princess…To even dream of such a thing!

CURDIE. *(struggling to speak)* Please…

LOOTIE. I won't listen to any more of your cheek! People like you should learn to know their place in the world!

*(***LOOTIE*** exits, after* **IRENE.***)*

CURDIE. Stupid and blind…All of them! All of them!

(a loud scream from off)

They have taken her… *(falls)*

(Enter **LOOTIE,** *terrified.)*

LOOTIE. Someone, come! Please, someone come! Guards! Guards!

(Enter **KING-PAPA** *and the* **CAPTAIN.***)*

Oh, your majesty…Something terrible has happened… Terrible!

KING-PAPA. Speak up, woman! What's the matter with you?

LOOTIE. They were waiting in the palace! They have stolen her away!

KING-PAPA. It can't be true!

LOOTIE. She fought and fought but they were too strong… They carried her down to the cellars…The goblins have her.

KING-PAPA. Call the guard! To the palace! To the cellars!

(Enter **KRANKL,** *safely on high.)*

KRANKL. Too late, your majesty!

KING-PAPA. Where is my daughter?

KRANKL. Where you will never find her! My creatures have taken her down deep into my kingdom. *(throws ring)* Here is the ring I took from her finger! She will wear no ring but mine, for I will make her my wife!

KING-PAPA. Never! Stand and fight!

KRANKL. Never! Prince Krankl bids you farewell.

KING-PAPA. I'll find her! Hear me, goblin!

(**KRANKL** *flees, laughing with triumph.*)

KING-PAPA. No-one ever escapes from the goblins...She is lost...

CAPTAIN. The boy...The boy spoke the truth.

KING-PAPA. Never to see her face, never to hear her voice... It will break my heart...

(**KING-PAPA** *goes, followed by the* **CAPTAIN**.)

LOOTIE. *(wiping her tears)* So the goblins have taken you, my little princess...*(with something like pleasure)* Just as I always said they would...Well, you'll have no-one running after you hand and foot now, my girl...No, no, you won't be so proud now...

(**LOOTIE** *goes*)

(**CURDIE** *lies abandoned and alone. Enter* **GREAT GRANDMOTHER**. *She takes up* **IRENE**'*s ring and goes to* **CURDIE**.)

GREAT GRANDMOTHER. The stars are spinning their threads
And the clouds are the dust that flies.
The moonlight weaves them up
For the time when your love shall rise.
The ocean in music rolls,
And a white bird calls and cries
To the mountain that waits in silence
For the time when your love shall rise.

Rise, now. Your wounds are healed. Get up onto your feet.

(**CURDIE** *rises to his feet.*)

CURDIE. I can see you...The Queen Of Light...*(rubs his eyes, shakes his head)* No, you are a dream...

GREAT GRANDMOTHER. Then dream often, Curdie Peterson, for there may be more truth in your dreams than your waking thoughts.

CURDIE. I am strong again! *(remembering)* But they have stolen her away! I must go and find the princess!

GREAT GRANDMOTHER. Yes, you must, for if you cannot find her then there is nothing I or the king or all his soldiers can do to save her.

CURDIE. I will save her! Only a miner knows the secrets of a mountain for it is his business to bring to light hidden things! I will go down into darkness and bring her up again into the light. Hear me, you thieves and cowards of the underworld – I have sworn it!

End of Act One

ACT TWO

Scene One

(The goblin palace, deep under the mountain.)

(Enter **PRINCESS IRENE**, *at a run.)*

IRENE. I've escaped! They'll never catch me now! I'll run and run…*(goes to run, but is prevented by the sound of laughter)* Goblins! I'll run this way! *(more laughter)* They're everywhere! I'll hide until they sleep, and then I'll find my way out…

(She backs towards the shadows. **CROWN PRINCE KRANKL**, *walking proudly with* **FANNON** *at his side, appears behind her.)*

KRANKL. Got you! *(She screams with fright.)* I let you run away so you would learn that you can never escape from me. Let that be your first lesson! *(takes her arm)* Behold my kingdom! For a thousand years the goblins have carved their way into the heart of the great mountain. The palace is huge and magnificent – Is it not the very wonder of the world?

IRENE. Your palace is dark and ugly and cold. *(shivers)* I cannot live here.

KRANKL. But you must, my little Irene, for it is your home now. How lucky you are! Soon I will marry you, and you will be my wife.

IRENE. Your wife! No, Prince Krankl – never!

KRANKL. I am a great catch! My like leap but once into the world and their first deeds declare their genius! You will be my princess, and one day you will be queen of the goblins!

IRENE. I would rather be queen of the frogs!

KRANKL. Mind your mouth, human! I will have respect from you!

IRENE. You're cruel, and you're a bully and you're a coward!

KRANKL. Why, thank-you.

IRENE. You won't keep me here! I'll escape, just you see if I don't!

KRANKL. In your dreams, and dreams hurt more than anything because dreams can never come true!

IRENE. I won't believe that!

KRANKL. It will be your next lesson, make no mistake, and I will be your teacher!…But I must go…I have gifts to bring you, gifts of welcome…And feel free to run away. You could wander these caverns for a hundred years and never find the sun.

IRENE. Go! Please go…but I ask one favour – take that horrible dragon with you!

KRANKL. Don't you like Fannon?

IRENE. I hate him. He's ugly and fierce and he scares me.

KRANKL. Since you hate him so much I think he had better…stay! *(laughs)* Stay, Fannon! Make her feel at home! *(FANNON roars.)* That's the way. Good boy! *(KRANKL exits, laughing.)*

IRENE. I knew if I asked for one thing, he would do the other. All cruel people are the same…You're a good dragon, aren't you? *(FANNON roars fiercely.)* Don't be angry, Fannon…*(He roars more loudly, comes towards her menacingly.)* Fannon? You do remember me, don't you? *(FANNON charges at her, roaring, flailing his wings.)* Fannon! Stop it! Please!

(She covers her eyes in terror, but FANNON rushes past her and flushes out SLY who has been hiding.)

The goblin spy!

(FANNON chases SLY.)

Good boy, Fannon! Chase him! Bite his legs! Go on! *(She watches as FANNON chases SLY off.)* Come back, Fannon! Don't leave me here on my own! Let him go. Please, come back. *(Enter FANNON.)* Good dragon. I thought you had forgotten me…We are friends, aren't we? *(FANNON gives a gentle roar.)* Come over here, then.

Come on. *(He goes to her and she strokes and pats him.)* Let me see your wing. *(She examines his wing.)* It's nearly all better now. Soon you'll be able to fly. *(***FANNON** *licks her.)* Stop licking! I'm glad I've found a friend. It's like I've been swallowed down into the belly of some huge monster…But you! You've been a prisoner in the dark for six years. Do you ever dream of the sun? Do you dream of a ball of fire hanging in the sky like a giant lamp? You keep dreaming, Fannon, and I'll take you out of here. I'll find a way, I promise! *(looks off)* He's coming back! Quickly, pretend to be fierce! As fierce as you can!

*(***FANNON** *roars murderously.* **IRENE** *cowers. Enter* **KRANKL***, holding a jewel-box.)*

KRANKL. *(approvingly)* That's my boy! *(to* **IRENE***)* My poor lamb, was he very vicious?

IRENE. Yes, he was.

KRANKL. I'm so glad. Here is my gift to you – the royal jewels. *(opens the box)* You may have anything you want.

IRENE. Anything?

KRANKL. All you have to do is ask.

IRENE. Then let me go away from here.

KRANKL. Anything but that!

IRENE. I'm asking you as hard as I can – let me go. You've got to because I'm not yours to keep.

*(***PRINCE KRANKL** *folds his arms and turns away.)*

I'll ask again. Please, Prince Krankl, let me go home.

KRANKL. Your eyes…How brave you are.

IRENE. Then you will let me go? You will, won't you?

KRANKL. Oh no, it's out of the question. Goblins never let anyone go.

*(***IRENE** *turns away from him.)*

What's the matter?

IRENE. *(near to tears)* I let myself hope…hope…

KRANKL. *(shakes his head, sighs)* Hopes and dreams, hopes and dreams…*(with quiet eagerness)* Are you going to cry?

IRENE. *(sensing his eagerness)* No! I hate to cry!

KRANKL. What a pity. *(holds up ring.)* And here is your wedding-ring!

IRENE. I will wear only one ring – the ring you tore from my finger!

KRANKL. You will wear this ring and you will be my wife!

IRENE. No!

KRANKL. Yes!

IRENE. No!

KRANKL. Yes!

IRENE. You can't make me!

KRANKL. Oh yes I can!

IRENE. *(together with **AUDIENCE**)* Oh no you can't!

KRANKL. Oh yes I can!

IRENE. *(together with **AUDIENCE**)* Oh no you can't! *(She stamps on his foot.)*

KRANKL. *(hopping in agony)* That's where you're wrong, you stupid little brats! *(recovers, advances menacingly on **IRENE**)* Goblins have secrets! Dark secrets about dark things that live in dark places! We have magic, little Irene, dark magic, black magic, strong magic!

IRENE. I'm not scared of you! *(goes to leave)*

KRANKL. You are so, I know you are! You want to run away from Prince Krankl…Then run! Go on! And remember – you will never find the way out!

*(**IRENE** goes.)*

Go after her, Fannon! Chase her! Bite her! Go on, boy!

*(**FANNON** roars and runs off after **IRENE**.)*

How pleased I am with my cruelty today. She is frightened and lonely and soon I will call on Banshee – The Dark Witch of The Mountain! She will use her magic to break the girl's spirit and then she will be mine – forever! You'll see, brats. Oh yes, you'll see!

*(**KRANKL** exits.)*

Scene Two

(The open mountainside. Night.)

(Enter **CURDIE** *with his* **MOTHER** *and* **FATHER**.*)*

FATHER. There, high in the rock – the doorway to their kingdom.

MOTHER. The cave hangs open like the mouth of some terrible beast.

FATHER. You must go deep into the very heart of the mountain.

CURDIE. Is that where they hold her – in the very heart?

FATHER. Yes.

CURDIE. Then that's where I must go.

MOTHER. No miner has gone so far into the darkness.

CURDIE. I would be less afraid, mother, if I knew you did not fear for me.

MOTHER. Then I put aside all weakness and fear. From this moment I am as brave as my son. But beware the goblins. Now that they have stolen the princess they will be stronger than ever.

FATHER. It's true – they will be fairly bursting with pride and mischief.

MOTHER. So keep your wits about you! Show no mercy if none is shown to you, and remember this – A new rhyme has more power than the old rhymes, but only if it is spoken from the heart.

CURDIE. I won't forget.

MOTHER. *(kisses him.)* No mother could wish for a better son, or princess a braver champion.

   *(***MOTHER** *goes.)*

FATHER. I will lead the miners to the goblins' tunnel. If you take the princess back from them they will be driven by spite to burst open the underground lake. We'll block up their tunnel and hold back their flood.

CURDIE. You'll do it.

FATHER. We'll try, we'll try…*(awkwardly)* So, you're ready then? *(***CURDIE** *nods.)* You're sure, now?

CURDIE. I'm sure.

FATHER. Do your best. No-one can ask more than that.

CURDIE. Yes, father.

FATHER. And you heard what your mother said?

CURDIE. I heard.

FATHER. It's hard to find the words…

CURDIE. Good luck to you, father.

FATHER. Good luck to you, son…Good luck.

(**FATHER** *goes.*)

CURDIE. Alone…I have no fear for myself, but what if I become lost and can't find her? The goblins will have her bones and I'll never see her again. It's a terrible thought and it steals away my courage.

(*Enter* **GREAT GRANDMOTHER.**)

GREAT GRANDMOTHER. Let your heart be brave.

(**CURDIE** *starts back in fear and wonder.*)

Come, boy – have you never seen the moonlight before?

CURDIE. Yes, but never without the moon.

GREAT GRANDMOTHER. You know me now.

CURDIE. You are The Queen Of Light, and without you I would be dead of my wounds.

GREAT GRANDMOTHER. The child is not meant to die, but to be forever fresh born. Are you ready?

CURDIE. I am ready.

GREAT GRANDMOTHER. But you do not know how you will find her.

CURDIE. You do, and that is enough.

GREAT GRANDMOTHER. Take back her ring to her.

(*She blows on her hand and* **IRENE***'s ring appears in his hand.*)

Keep it on your finger. Its magic thread led her to you and now it may lead you to her.

CURDIE. Her ring…(*puts it on his finger*) But I can't see any thread.

GREAT GRANDMOTHER. You must learn to believe without seeing.

CURDIE. I can't do that.

GREAT GRANDMOTHER. How do you know until you try?

CURDIE. *(feeling with his ringfinger)* There's something…A breath on my finger…Her soft hair…My imagination…

GREAT GRANDMOTHER. Trust the ring!

CURDIE. I will try to do as you say…You make me strong.

GREAT GRANDMOTHER. Go now, Curdie Peterson. *(He goes.)* May her ring kindle a flame inside him to light his way in the darkness of the great mountain.

Scene Four

(The goblin palace. Enter **PRINCESS IRENE** *and* **FANNON**.*)*

IRENE. These tunnels go on for ever and ever. I'm sure we're going round in circles, but we have to keep looking or we'll never find a way out. *(strokes* **FANNON***)* You really are the best dragon in the whole world...And your wings are so beautiful. Perhaps one day you will let me sit on your back and we'll fly over oceans, forests and mountains...But remember and pretend to be fierce! *(She roars and* **FANNON** *roars back.)* Fiercer! *(He roars more fiercely.)* That's the way. They would never let me keep you if they knew you were my friend. Come on, then – we've got to keep looking. One day, Fannon, you'll see the sun rising in the sky. I promise.

*(***IRENE** *exits with* **FANNON**.*)*

(Enter **SLY**, *hissing with pleasure at having discovered* **FANNON**'s *treason. He goes after them.)*

(Enter **CROWN PRINCE KRANKL**, **KING COB** *and* **QUEEN MAM** *wheeling a huge gong.)*

QUEEN MAM. We'll use the golden gong of the goblins to call up The Witch Banshee from the depths of the earth.

KRANKL. Her magic will make Irene my wife!

QUEEN MAM. She is the luckiest of girls.

KING COB. I just hope the witch doesn't get angry...You know how she hates to be disturbed.

QUEEN MAM. *(stamps on his foot)* Don't be such a worry-worm! Hurry up and bong it!

KING COB. Bong it yourself!

QUEEN MAM. You bong it!

KING COB. You're the worry-worm! You bong the gong!

(They all grimace in pain and hold their ears.)

QUEEN MAM. Watch your tongue – that rhymed!

KING COB. Well, I don't see why I should be the one who has to bong it!

QUEEN MAM. You're the king!

KING COB. You're the queen!

QUEEN MAM. Stop arguing and bong the gong! *(They grimace in pain and hold their ears.)* Oh my poor head...I'll bong you, you stupid-looking...

KRANKL. Out of my way! I'll bong the...!!! I will strike the sacred artefact! Three times it must be struck to call her to my side!

QUEEN MAM. Oh brilliant boy!

*(*KRANKL* strikes the gong and* MAM *and* COB *vibrate to its deep resonance.)*

KRANKL. Hail Banshee, Queen Of Darkness and Cruellest Of All! Hear thy servants! *(Strikes the gong. An evil wind gets up.)* Come, Great Witch, come forth to our goblin-hall! *(Strikes the gong. The evil wind grows stronger.)* Behold, the Dark Mistress of the Mountain! *(He points, and they all look off.)* She comes, she comes!

(The terrifying form of **BANSHEE** *appears behind them, vexed to discover that they are looking the wrong way. She gestures and there is an explosion of purple smoke. The goblins fall to the ground with fright, and cower before her.)*

BANSHEE. *(furious)* Who dares to call Banshee to their side!?

QUEEN MAM

KING COB. *(in unison, pointing at* KRANKL*)* It was him! It was him!

BANSHEE. Well, speak up, boy, or my cat shall have your tongue!

KRANKL. M-mighty witch, I wish you to help me.

BANSHEE. I am a goblin-witch, and I help no-one but myself!

KRANKL. Help me with my cruelty?

BANSHEE. I've told you...Cruelty, did you say?

KRANKL. Yes, great one, and who better to ask since you are the Cruellest Of All?

BANSHEE. True, true. I've always been partial to cruelty, especially to children! *(discovers* AUDIENCE*)* Children! What are they doing down here?

KING COB. They get everywhere!

BANSHEE. I hate children more than anything in the world! They're so stupid they can't even feed themselves without making a mess all over the table! Smelly, revolting little worms! Oh yes you are!

AUDIENCE. Oh no we're not!

BANSHEE, GOBLINS. *(in unison)* Oh yes you are!

AUDIENCE. Oh no we're not!

BANSHEE. The cheek of them! To answer back to a witch!

QUEEN MAM. My hand's itching!

BANSHEE. I've got to hurt them! I must, I must!

KRANKL. I know how, great witch. We have stolen a sun-girl, a princess. They're on her side, so if you hurt the princess then you hurt them too.

BANSHEE. Perfect! Tell me more!

KRANKL. I want to make her marry me.

BANSHEE. Wonderful! She will be miserable for the rest of her life!

KRANKL. But first she must agree to be my wife.

BANSHEE. Let my magic be your priest. Here, boy, take this cup.

*(**KRANKL** takes the golden goblet from her.)*

It is my witch's-cup and has great power. Now, listen, and you will hear what you must do. Make her cry! Make her cry, and you must catch her tears in the witch's-cup. Drink her tears and she is bound by magic to be your bride.

KRANKL. I will have her cry such tears as will drown her pride in a river of sorrow!

KING COB. She will cry her heart out!

QUEEN MAM. We will catch it in the cup!

KRANKL. I will drink from the cup and she will be mine, mine!

BANSHEE. What a wedding it will be! I myself will perform the ceremony.

KRANKL. *(bows low)* My thanks, great witch. It will be a great honour.

BANSHEE. Just so long as I can get at them! *(indicates* **AUDI-ENCE***)* Pathetic little cry-babies! Go on – shout all you like. It will only make hurting the princess all the more enjoyable! See you at the wedding! Away! *(There is an explosion, and she vanishes.)*

QUEEN MAM. All we must do is make her cry.

KING COB. Easy, easy, easy!

KRANKL. No, father! She is stronger than she looks! I must be at my very best. I wonder…

(enter **SLY***)*

Welcome, Sly. What news for your master?

*(***SLY*** whispers in his ear.)*

Oh sweet spy, now am I sure of success for you have given me the key to a secret door.

KING COB. *(looking off)* The girl! The girl is coming!

QUEEN MAM. She walks in circles, the little fool!

KRANKL. *(to* **SLY***)* To the shadows! (***SLY*** *withdraws into dark-ness.)* I will keep the cup ready. I have a thirst and soon I must drink!

(enter **IRENE** *and* **FANNON***.)*

Princess Irene, your family bids you welcome.

IRENE. My family?

QUEEN MAM. From now on you must think of me as your mother.

KING COB. And me as your father. Call me Papa.

QUEEN MAM. Call me Mama.

IRENE. Never!

QUEEN MAM. We're not good enough for her! Don't you like us, dearie?

IRENE. The only thing I like about you is your shoes!

QUEEN MAM. My shoes?

KRANKL, KING COB. *(in unison)* Her shoes?

IRENE. Yes, her shoes. They're neat on, as my nurse might say, and I would like a pair the very same.

QUEEN MAM. Such taste in one so young…I will have a pair made for you, my dear.

IRENE. How kind…And then I can hide my toes like you do.

QUEEN MAM. Of course you may…What did you say!

IRENE. I can hide my toes like you do.

QUEEN MAM. Toes! Toes!…*(holds her head)* This is too much… I shall have to go.

KRANKL. *(gently)* Stay, mother. *(to* **IRENE***)* How dare you be rude to my mother the queen!

QUEEN MAM. I feel quite faint.

KRANKL. My mother does not have toes on her feet!

IRENE. Oh yes she does!

GOBLINS. Oh no she doesn't!

IRENE. *(with* **AUDIENCE***)* Oh yes she does!

GOBLINS. Oh no she doesn't!

IRENE. *(with* **AUDIENCE***)* Oh yes she does!

QUEEN MAM. *(silencing* **KRANKL** *and* **COB***'s response)* That's it…I've heard enough…I'm going…I'm going…*(She goes, in a state.)*

KRANKL. Now look what you've done! *(draws sword)* I'll teach you respect! (**KRANKL** *attacks* **IRENE***, but* **FANNON** *protects her, roaring threateningly.)* But what's this, I wonder?

IRENE. *(quickly)* It's nothing. You gave him a fright, that's all.

KRANKL. Oh no, I don't think so. (**KRANKL** *makes another attack, but* **FANNON** *roars and advances forcing* **KRANKL** *to back away.)* Faithless beast!

IRENE. Oh Fannon, now he knows you're my friend. *(forgives him with a hug)*

KRANKL. Of course, I knew all the time.

IRENE. How did you know?

KING COB. Perhaps a little bird told him.

(Enter **SLY***, hissing with pleasure.)*

IRENE. Your horrible spy!

KRANKL. So you see, princess, there is nothing I do not know.

*(**FANNON** chases **SLY**, who hides behind **KRANKL**.)*

Traitor! *(brandishes his sword)*

IRENE. Leave him alone!

KRANKL. You tried to trick me, and no-one ever tricks Prince Krankl!

IRENE. Please don't hurt him!

KING COB. Oh we'll hurt him all right! *(waves his sword)* We'll clip his wings!

KRANKL. Catch him, father!

*(They chase **FANNON** with their swords.)*

KING COB. I've got him, I've got him! *(collides with **KRANKL**)*

IRENE. Run, Fannon, run! *(He comes to her.)* Don't worry about me! Run, go on! Run!

*(**FANNON** eludes his chasers, and runs off.)*

KRANKL. Don't think he has escaped me! Soon we will hunt him by torchlight. We will ride on our pigs and hunt him down with our knives and arrows. We will kill him for our sport!

*(**IRENE** hangs her head in sorrow.)*

Look, father – the little princess is very, very sad.

KING COB. How lonely she will be without her friend the dragon.

KRANKL. And her so far away from home.

KING COB. So far, far away from home.

KRANKL. *(producing witch's-cup, behind **IRENE**'s back)* I hope she's not going to cry.

IRENE. I am not going to cry!

*(**KRANKL** hides the witch's cup.)*

I wouldn't give you the satisfaction! Leave me! Go on – leave me alone!

KRANKL. Very well, Princess Irene, I must go and get ready for our wedding! *(bows)* I leave you alone with darkness and fear. But you will find me in the great hall. You can always run to me if you want a shoulder to cry on.

*(**KRANKL** laughs and goes with **SLY** and **KING COB**, who wheels the gong.)*

IRENE. Oh, Fannon, I miss you already…I try to be brave but it only gets harder and harder. It's so dark and I'm so alone. *(shivers)* I'll never escape from here? I'll never see the sun rise again over the mountain…never…

VOICE. Let your heart be brave.

IRENE. Who's there! Show yourself!

GREAT GRANDMOTHER. Here, Irene.

IRENE. You've come! You've really come…But I can hardly see you.

GREAT GRANDMOTHER. A queen of light has little power in the kingdom of darkness.

IRENE. If you were truly a queen of light you would blast this place with all your brightness and beauty!

GREAT GRANDMOTHER. I have no magic for that, but still I mean to help you.

IRENE. Help me! You tell me to be as brave as a tiger and go out into the world, but look how I'm a prisoner in the dark! And soon I must be married to the prince of the goblins! I should have listened to my nurse. How can you help me?

GREAT GRANDMOTHER. Listen, and I will tell you! Lift up your head and go to the goblins! Warn them that they must let you go, or they will be punished for their crimes! Tell them a great power is coming to their palace, a power greater than all their cruelty and magic put together!

IRENE. What great power, and how can the weak give warning to the strong? They'll laugh at me.

GREAT GRANDMOTHER. Let them laugh, if that is their choice. *(withdraws)* Trust me.

IRENE. Wait, Great Grandmother…Don't go…

GREAT GRANDMOTHER. Trust me.

(**GREAT GRANDMOTHER** *vanishes.*)

IRENE. I'll try to trust you, for the sake of all your kindness…I'll do what you say, Great Grandmother – one last time!

(**IRENE** *goes.*)

Scene Four

(The goblin mines, deep under the great mountain.)

(Enter CURDIE, following the thread.)

CURDIE. I've walked for miles and miles but I've found nothing! Magic thread! All I've done is follow my imagination straight to the heart of nowhere! But how else can I find her? *(feels for thread.)* No – I'm done with that! I'm sorry, Princess Irene, I'd save you if I could, but I'm lost and I'll never find you...

(a deep roar from off)

What's that sound? It's no goblin I ever heard! *(brandishes pickaxe)* Don't hide in the dark! Come on, whoever you are! Show yourself!

(Enter FANNON, roaring.)

I'll show you, if it's a fight you're after!...Wait, I know you...You're Fannon. She came right up to you and pulled the spike from your wing...She wasn't scared... It is you, isn't it? *(puts out his hand)* Here boy. Good boy. *(FANNON goes to him.)* I never thought I'd see anyone ever again. *(pats him)* You're a great big lump, so you are. *(FANNON licks him.)* Stop licking! *(FANNON gives a friendly roar.)* But maybe you could lead me to her! Could you, Fannon, could you lead me to Princess Irene? *(FANNON roars, and exits.)* Good dragon, Fannon! Wait for me! Wait for me! *(He exits after FANNON.)*

Scene Five

(The great-hall in the goblin palace. Enter KING COB *and* QUEEN MAM, *wheeling their gong. They are dressed as for a wedding.)*

QUEEN MAM. *(showing off her dress)* Well?

KING COB. Well what?

QUEEN MAM. *(stamps on his foot)* Well, don't you think I look beautiful?!

KING COB. *(hopping in agony)* Beautiful, my queen...Magnificent!

QUEEN MAM. How kind. I do so enjoy a wedding.

(enter PRINCE KRANKL *in his wedding-suit.)*

And our son! *(to* AUDIENCE*)* Don't you think he's the most handsome prince in all the world?

AUDIENCE. No!

GOBLINS. *(in unison)* Oh yes he is!

AUDIENCE. Oh no he's not!

KRANKL. Silence, brats! *(points to* KING.*)* When he's dead I'll be king of the goblins!

KING COB. You tell them, son!...Eh?

QUEEN MAM. And after he's married the princess, he'll be king of the humans too!

KRANKL. *(to* AUDIENCE*)* So mind your manners, or I'll have you locked up!

KING COB. *(looking off)* Here she comes! Here comes the bride!

KRANKL. And still no tears...How brave she is.

QUEEN MAM. *(rolling up her sleeves)* She must be made to cry!

KRANKL. Leave her, mother, leave her to me.

(enter IRENE.*)*

My dear princess. *(offers an embrace)* You have come to your prince.

IRENE. *(turning away)* Listen to me, Prince Krankl, for I have something very important to say.

KRANKL. No! I must speak first, I insist! Sweet princess, I wish to say…This is hard for me…I wish to say that I am sorry.

IRENE. Sorry? You?

KRANKL. Yes…What a monster I have become. It was wrong of me to steal you away and keep you prisoner, I know that now.

KING COB. He's cracked, he's flipped his lid!

QUEEN MAM. Are you ill, my son?

KRANKL. *(to his parents)* Silence! You should be ashamed to have such a son as I! Ashamed! *(to* **IRENE.***)* Your eyes… Still they shine with a thousand dreams of happiness… And now you have made me dream too…I dream of being as brave and good as you are…Princess Irene, can you ever forgive me?

IRENE. I could, Prince Krankl, if I could ever believe you.

KRANKL. How can I make you believe me?…I know what I must do – I will spare the dragon.

IRENE. Oh please…Do you promise?

KRANKL. I promise, and I shall give him to you as a gift.

IRENE. Thank-you, Prince Krankl.

KRANKL. How lovely to see your smile…And of course, I must let you go.

QUEEN MAM. It can't be true!

KING COB. Goblins never let anyone go! I won't allow it!

KRANKL. You will do as I say! She is my prisoner and I will let her go if I want! *(to* **IRENE.***)* You are free. Go on, princess, go back to your home, and try to forgive me.

IRENE. You mean it, don't you?

KRANKL. You silly girl, of course I mean it.

IRENE. Perhaps one day we'll be friends…True friends.

KRANKL. I'd like that very much.

IRENE. I believe you. *(kisses him on the cheek)* Goodbye, Prince Krankl, and thank you…*(goes to leave, stops)* I don't know my way…Who will guide me home?

KRANKL. Father?

KING COB. Of course…Except I have work to do.

KRANKL. Mother?

QUEEN MAM. Of course…Except I am needed in the kitchen.

(IRENE looks to KRANKL. KING COB and QUEEN MAM burst into loud laughter.)

KING COB, QUEEN MAM. *(in unison, through laughter)* She believed him! She really believed him!

IRENE. No!…*(goes to KRANKL)* You didn't lie to me…Tell me you didn't lie…Prince Krankl?

KRANKL. Of course I lied! You little fool!

(IRENE hangs her head.)

How could you be so stupid? Hope cuts the deepest wounds! This the goblins have always known, and now you have learned it for yourself!

(IRENE hides her head in her hands.)

KING COB. Quickly, she has to cry now!

QUEEN MAM. The stupid little cry-baby!

KRANKL. *(producing the witch's-cup)* The witch's-cup will be filled to the brim!

(The goblins gather and slowly approach IRENE, eagerly holding out the witch's-cup.)

GOBLINS. *(in unison, rising from a whisper)* She's going to cry, she's going to cry, she's going to cry, she's going to cry!

IRENE. *(rounds on them, ablaze with fury)* That's what you think! You lie and you cheat and you steal but I don't care because I've got something to say and you'd better listen because if you don't it'll be the worse for you! A great power is coming to your palace, greater than anything you could ever know or understand! So I'm giving you a warning – let me go or you'll be punished for all your meanness and cruelty! You'll be punished so you won't be able to hurt anyone ever again! And don't say you haven't been warned!

*(The **GOBLINS** look around fearfully, but slowly relax when nothing appears to harm them.)*

QUEEN MAM. *(feeling herself)* Nothing.

KING COB. *(feeling himself)* I'm still in one piece.

KRANKL. *(to* **IRENE***)* A warning! Ha! You're an even bigger fool than I thought!

(The **GOBLINS** *begin to laugh.)*

IRENE. *(near to tears)* They're laughing at me…

KRANKL. There's nothing…*(Laughs.)*

IRENE. Where are you?…Where are you?

KRANKL. Absolutely nothing!

CURDIE. *(entering)* I'm here, Irene.

GOBLINS. *(in unison)* You!!!!

IRENE. Curdie Peterson…I've hoped and hoped…*(runs to him)*

CURDIE. How happy I am to find you.

KRANKL. *(sneering)* This is your great power!

QUEEN MAM. There's more power in my little finger!

CURDIE. I've come to take the princess home.

KING COB. In your dreams!

KRANKL. We'll finish you this time, miner-boy!

(They advance on **CURDIE** *and* **IRENE.** **CURDIE** *gives a whistle and* **FANNON** *enters taking his place beside them, and forcing the* **GOBLINS** *to retreat.* **KING COB** *and* **KRANKL** *draw their swords.)*

KRANKL. Let battle commence!

CURDIE. Let battle commence!

*(***CURDIE** *closes with* **KRANKL,** *and* **FANNON** *with* **KING COB.** **QUEEN MAM** *charges at* **IRENE,** *stamping her granite shoes.)*

QUEEN MAM. I'll teach you about shoes, girl!

*(***IRENE** *catches hold of* **QUEEN MAM***'s foot, forcing* **MAM** *to hop helplessly.)*

IRENE. No, queen – it is I who will teach you!

CURDIE. Go on, Irene!

(They all stop fighting and watch in amazement.)

QUEEN MAM. No, no!

IRENE. Come one and all, come let it be seen,
What grows on the feet of the goblin-queen!

(**IRENE** *wrenches off the shoe, to reveal her toes.* **KRANKL** *and* **KING COB** *stare in disbelief.*)

KRANKL. Toes!!! Oh, Mother, how could you? *(retches)*

(**CURDIE** *takes* **IRENE**'s *hand, she touches* **FANNON**'s *wing, and they all begin to creep away.*)

QUEEN MAM. I know...They're disgusting...

KING COB. You mean you've had toes on your feet all these years and you've never told me!

QUEEN MAM. Yes, yes It's all true...

KING COB. But I love toes! *(kneels, holds her foot)*

QUEEN MAM. What!

KING COB. They're beautiful! Think how happy we could have been if only you had told me!

QUEEN MAM. I'll go mad...Mad!

KRANKL. They're escaping! You'll pay for this!

CURDIE. Quickly, Irene!

(*He backs away, but* **SLY** *appears behind him.*)

IRENE. The spy, Curdie!

(*She pulls him away just in time to avoid* **SLY**'s *poisonous bite.*)

KRANKL. *(to* **SLY***)* Fool!

(**FANNON** *rushes at* **SLY**, *chases him.*)

IRENE. Good boy, Fannon! That's the way! (**FANNON** *chases* **SLY** *off.* **IRENE** *calls after him.*) Catch him this time, and don't let him go!

CURDIE. We'll go after him.

QUEEN MAM. That's what you think! *(strikes the gong)*

KRANKL. Genius!

CURDIE. What's she doing?

QUEEN MAM. Come, Banshee! Hear your servants! *(strikes the gong)*

IRENE. I don't like this!

GOBLINS. *(in unison)* Come, great one – come!

> *(***QUEEN MAM*** strikes the third blow and ***BANSHEE*** appears, by magic.)*

BANSHEE. Banshee hears your call!

IRENE. It's a witch!

CURDIE. Quickly, Irene – run!

BANSHEE. Be still, boy! *(***BANSHEE*** gestures and ***CURDIE*** is held by her spell.)*

CURDIE. I can't move! I can't move a muscle!

IRENE. She's put a spell on you!

BANSHEE. *(to* ***IRENE,*** *stroking her face.)* So you are the princess. What a sweet and pretty little bride you will make.

IRENE. No!

BANSHEE. Yes, yes! But never mind, you'll feel all the better for a good cry…A good cry and you'll be as right as rain.

IRENE. *(near to tears)* Help me, Curdie.

KRANKL. Well, aren't you going to help her?

QUEEN MAM. *(mockingly)* Let's have some of your gobble-gobble-gobble.

KING COB. Or your hobble-hobble-hobble.

KRANKL. We've heard all your old rhymes. They won't help you now!

CURDIE. *(struggling against the spell)* Let me go!

BANSHEE. Never! I have come to perform a wedding and a wedding there will be!

> *(***QUEEN MAM*** hauls ***IRENE*** to ***KRANKL***'s side.)*

KRANKL. *(to* ***CURDIE***) And you can be best-man and watch while the princess marries Prince Krankl, the husband she hates and fears most in the whole world! *(Produces witch's cup.)*

BANSHEE. Oh perfect love! Let the ceremony begin!

IRENE. I'm going to cry…cry…

KRANKL. My poor dear girl.

CURDIE. No, Irene…I have a new rhyme, and it is for you.

BANSHEE. A new rhyme! Stop him!

CURDIE. Once I dreamed of winds and sea
　　And great ships sailing fast and free,
　　But now I dream of you, my love;
　　You are my ship, you are my sea.

　　*(The **GOBLINS** hold their heads and twist in agony.)*

BANSHEE. *(shaking with fear and pain)* A love-rhyme – the
　　strongest magic of all!

CURDIE. I've mined this rock for stones most rare,
　　Diamonds bright, and rubies fair,
　　But none so rare as you, my love;
　　Not one to you could I compare.

　　*(**CURDIE** breaks free of the spell.)*

QUEEN MAM. *(clinging giddily to **KRANKL**)* I'll be sick! *(to
　　KING COB)* Fetch the bucket!

　　*(**KING COB** runs in a drunken fashion to obey.)*

BANSHEE. *(Screams.)* My head, my head…It's going to explode!

　　*(**IRENE** goes to **CURDIE**.)*

CURDIE. Now is the time for our love to rise
　　Up from this prison, out under the skies
　　To the sun that warms the world above;
　　Come live with me and be my love.

IRENE. I will, Curdie Peterson…I will.

　　*(The **GOBLINS** are sick in their bucket. **BANSHEE** wails
　　and shakes and steams.)*

CURDIE. Look out! I think she's going to…

　　*(**BANSHEE** explodes and vanishes in a cloud of purple
　　smoke.)*

IRENE. You've beaten the witch!

CURDIE. We're free, Irene…free… *(They run off.)*

KRANKL. *(Shouting after them.)* Come back here! I order you
　　to come back! I am Prince of the Mountain! Come
　　back! I command it!

(QUEEN MAM takes the witch's-cup from him, and cries into it.)

KING COB. Gone away…

QUEEN MAM. *(weeping)* Gone away…

KRANKL. I've lost her…lost her…

KING COB. We've only ourselves to blame. We were too confident.

KRANKL. Oh what do you know, you old pig!

KING COB. I'll have none of your lip!

KRANKL. Tremble, tremble…Look at you, the pair of you! Idiots, idiots!

KING COB. I'll smack your mouth!

KRANKL. It's a miracle I've turned out as well as I have!

KING COB. I'll turn you out, pal! Inside out! *(Goes for him but is held back by QUEEN MAM.)*

QUEEN MAM. Stop it! Stop it!…I'm sure other families don't go through this. We must stick together…Together! *(points at AUDIENCE)* Look at them!

KING COB. The smirking little brats!

KRANKL. They're laughing because they think the Princess and the miner-boy have escaped from the mountain, but we know different, don't we, father?

KING COB. Of course, my lad!…Eh?

(KRANKL mimes an explosion.)

Of course – the lake!

QUEEN MAM. My brilliant boy!

KRANKL. We'll blow open the great underground lake and the water will rush down the tunnel in a mighty flood! The Princess and her boy will be drowned.

KING COB. And then the huge waterfall will erupt into the valley!

KRANKL. And the humans will be swept away and drowned! Each and every one of them!

KING COB. I can't wait!

QUEEN MAM. Hurry, then!

KRANKL. *(to* **AUDIENCE***)* So you see, brats, goblins never lose. *(He steps in bucket.)*

(Exeunt **GOBLINS***.)*

(Enter **CURDIE** *and* **IRENE***.)*

CURDIE. *(calling)* Fannon, come on, Fannon!

IRENE. *(calling)* Fannon, where are you? *(to* **CURDIE***)* We can't leave him down here.

CURDIE. I know. *(calls)* Fannon, come with us. Hurry!

IRENE. You can feel the hot sun on your wings…Oh, please come…

(The sound of a loud explosion.)

CURDIE. They have blown open the underground lake!

IRENE. Fannon! We must keep looking.

CURDIE. No, Irene! Listen! *(the sound of rushing water)* They have sent a flood after us!

IRENE. We'll be drowned!

CURDIE. Follow the thread, and run, run for your life! *(They run off.)*

(The sound of the rushing torrent swells and surges. Enter the **GOBLINS***, thrilled, gloating.)*

KRANKL. Run, river, run! Seize them in your mighty fist and carry them down to the very depths of the earth!

QUEEN MAM. *(with mock tears)* Bye-bye, little Princess. *(blows kiss, laughs)*

KING COB. What a pity. *(laughs)*

KRANKL. Her eyes…If I can't have her then no-one can have her! *(rounds on* **AUDIENCE***)* Let that be a lesson to you!

GOBLINS. *(to* **AUDIENCE***, in unison)* We're bigger, we're braver, we're better than you! Oh yes we are!

AUDIENCE. Oh no you're not!

QUEEN MAM. Listen to them!

KING COB. Pathetic!

GOBLINS. *(in unison)* We're better than you all!

(The sound of the rushing waters changes tone. The mountain shakes and trembles.)

QUEEN MAM. *(frightened)* What's going on?

KRANKL. Don't be afraid, mother. My plan is perfect.

(Again the mountain shakes and trembles.)

KING COB. *(looking off)* Look there! The flood has been turned back!

KRANKL. Impossible!

QUEEN MAM. *(pointing off)* It's coming this way! A huge wave! It's coming for us!

KING COB. We'll be swept away! Run! Me first, me first!

GOBLINS. *(in unison, clawing at each other, holding each other back)* Out of the way! Me first, me first, me first…Me, me, me, me, me, me, me!

(The sound of the rushing torrent grows louder.)

KRANKL. Too late! The flood is upon us! It's to the depths we must go! *(to AUDIENCE)* Horrible brats!

GOBLINS. *(to AUDIENCE, in unison)* The goblins hate you! We hate you all!

(Screaming in rage and terror, they are swept away by a mighty flood.)

Scene Six

(The open mountainside. First light. The sun is still behind the great mountain. The ground continues to rumble and shake.)

(Enter **KING-PAPA***.)*

KING-PAPA. *(Calling out.)* Irene! Where are you? Irene!

(Enter **NURSE LOOTIE***.)*

LOOTIE. Come inside, your majesty. You've stood all night on the mountain and are near dead from the cold.

KING-PAPA. Irene!…She may hear my voice and that may give her comfort. Irene! Irene!

(The ground is shaken by another rumbling quake.)

LOOTIE. *(terrified)* Listen to the ground. The world is coming to an end?

KING-PAPA. My little girl…To think that she is down there!

LOOTIE. Come inside, your majesty.

KING-PAPA. I won't leave her!

LOOTIE. I don't mean to be cruel, but you know as well as I – the goblins never give up their prisoners. You'll never see her again…*(takes his arm)* There now…Come with me…Come with me…*(She begins to lead him away.)*

(Enter **PRINCESS IRENE** *and* **CURDIE,** *unseen by* **LOOTIE** *and* **KING-PAPA. IRENE** *and* **CURDIE** *hold hands, following the thread together.)*

IRENE. Father?

KING-PAPA. Who's there – the wind?

IRENE. It's me, father – Irene.

LOOTIE. It can't be!

KING-PAPA. Come closer, girl…It is you! Irene! *(He embraces her.)* I thought I'd lost you forever!

IRENE. It's lovely to see you again, father.

KING-PAPA. Come with me to the palace…The servants will bring everything you wish…You can sleep in your own room again.

IRENE. *(gently)* No, Father…*(goes to* **CURDIE***)* I will not come with you.

LOOTIE. *(recognising* **CURDIE***)* You! Outrageous!

KING-PAPA. Who is this boy?

CURDIE. I'm Peter's son.

KING-PAPA. Who's Peter?

CURDIE. Peter the miner.

KING-PAPA. I don't know him.

CURDIE. I'm his son, though.

LOOTIE. The cheek of him!

IRENE. His name is Curdie Peterson, and he has saved me from the goblins.

KING-PAPA. Then he has done the impossible. *(to* **CURDIE***)* But I do know you…You gave me warning and I did not listen.

CURDIE. *(with a small bow)* Your majesty.

LOOTIE. *(taking* **IRENE***'s arm)* Stop your nonsense, and come home where it is safe.

IRENE. Let go of me, nurse Lootie.

LOOTIE. *(Letting go.)* Where will you go?

CURDIE. We will cross the great mountain…

IRENE. Yes, and walk down into the far countries of the world.

LOOTIE. Fiddlesticks!

IRENE. We have found a way.

LOOTIE. No-one has ever crossed the great mountain.

KING-PAPA. Then perhaps they will be the first.

LOOTIE. Your majesty?

KING-PAPA. Irene, do you want to go with this boy?

IRENE. Oh yes, father, I do.

KING-PAPA. Then I will not keep you here, for he has cared for you better than I.

*(***IRENE*** kisses him. He turns to* ***CURDIE***.)*

KING-PAPA. How can I thank you enough? Curdie Peterson, you are braver than any I have known born in castle or palace. I give you my thanks, and I give you my daughter. Keep her safe.

CURDIE. I will, sir.

KING-PAPA. I wish you luck. *(turns back to* **IRENE***)* Goodbye then, Irene.

IRENE. Goodbye, Father. *(hugs him)* Thank you for all you have given to me.

*(***KING-PAPA*** goes.)*

And thank you most of all for not trying to keep me here.

LOOTIE. *(to* **CURDIE***)* And as for you...There's more to you than meets the eye, miner-boy...Just remember and mind your manners! *(turns to* **IRENE***)* So, my little Irene, you're free of me at last...We've never much liked each other...No, no, it's as well to speak the truth...But I'll miss you all the same.

IRENE. And I'll miss you too, Lootie.

LOOTIE. Away with you! Your strict and stupid old nurse?

IRENE. My dear old nurse. *(embraces her)*

LOOTIE. *(through tears)* You'll come back and see us one day?

IRENE. Of course I will.

LOOTIE. You're a good girl when you try...a good girl...

*(***LOOTIE*** goes.)*

IRENE. *(fighting off tears)* All the goblins couldn't make me cry, but my own people!...

CURDIE. *(points off)* Look, Irene! The miners are coming out of the mountain. They are the real heroes.

IRENE. Why? I don't understand.

CURDIE. The goblins blew open the lake, you heard the explosion, but the miners had blocked their tunnel. Their work has saved us all!

(Enter **CURDIE***'s* **MOTHER** *and* **FATHER***.)*

CURDIE. Mother, Father!

(He runs and embraces them.)

MOTHER. You are safe... *(goes to* **IRENE***)* He found you.

IRENE. Yes, he did, in all that terrible darkness.

MOTHER. Just as you once found him.

CURDIE. I have asked Irene to come with me across the mountain.

FATHER. The mountain?

IRENE. We know our way.

FATHER. Who would doubt that now?

MOTHER. You must be together. Look how you have been saviours to each other. I wish you every happiness. *(embraces* **IRENE***)*

CURDIE. But father, what of the goblins?

FATHER. Our wall turned back their flood on their own palace and they were swept away! They have been punished by their own cruelty!

*(***IRENE*** *hangs her head in sorrow.)*

What's the matter, princess? They deserved nothing less.

IRENE. I know…but we have lost a very dear friend.

CURDIE. Were they all swept away?

FATHER. Yes, all except one who was strong enough to fight against the current. *(calls off)* Come on, then. This way…

IRENE. *(closing her eyes)* Oh please let it be him!

(Enter **FANNON***.)*

CURDIE. Fannon!

IRENE. *(opening her eyes)* It is you!

*(***CURDIE*** *and* **IRENE** *rush to him.)*

FATHER. He's beautiful! He must go with you on your journey.

MOTHER. If any cliff proves too high you may ride on his back and he will fly you to where you want to go.

IRENE. *(stroking him)* Do you hear, Fannon? You can come with us. *(***FANNON*** *gives a happy roar.)*

CURDIE. We have one last thing to do. *(takes* **IRENE***'s hand)*

IRENE. Follow the thread to its end.

(Together they follow the thread. **GREAT GRAND-MOTHER** *enters and comes to them.* **CURDIE'S MOTHER** *and* **FATHER** *start back in fear and wonder.)*

FATHER. The Queen of Light!

GREAT GRANDMOTHER. *(to* **MOTHER** *and* **FATHER***)* Do not be afraid. I come only to say farewell to our children.

MOTHER. We are not afraid.

GREAT GRANDMOTHER. *(to* **CURDIE** *and* **IRENE**) Well now, it's time you were on your way.

IRENE. Will I lose you now?

GREAT GRANDMOTHER. How can you lose me when I am your own?

IRENE. I'll never forget you.

GREAT GRANDMOTHER. Then you shall never be forgotten. *(The sun begins to rise.)* The sun!

IRENE. There, Fannon, your first sun is rising in the sky… It's lovely! Can you feel it's warmth on your wings? (**FANNON** *lazily stretches his wings.*)

(**CURDIE** *takes the ring from his finger.*)

GREAT GRANDMOTHER. *(to* **CURDIE**) Well, what are you waiting for?

CURDIE. Princess Irene, I must give you back your ring… *(puts it on her finger)* There – it is done.

IRENE. *(kisses the ring)* My own ring…Once, Curdie Peterson, I promised you a kiss…I will kiss you now…If you wish it…

CURDIE. I wish it.

(They kiss.)

GREAT GRANDMOTHER. Seek that your sons and your daughters may dream dreams and see visions. Seek that they may see true visions and dream noble dreams!…Go on your way.

FATHER. Goodbye, Curdie.

MOTHER. Goodbye, Irene.

CURDIE, IRENE. *(in unison)* Goodbye…

(Exeunt **MOTHER** *and* **FATHER**.*)*

GREAT GRANDMOTHER. Go now…We have come from a long, long way away and we have a great distance still to go…Goodbye, my children…

(**GREAT GRANDMOTHER** *goes.*)

CURDIE AND IRENE. *(in unison)* Goodbye… *(to* **AUDIENCE**) Goodbye, everyone…Goodbye…

(**CURDIE** *and* **IRENE**, *together of course with* **FANNON**, *turn and go towards the great mountain.*)

MUSIC USE NOTE

Licensees are solely responsible for obtaining formal written permission from copyright owners to use copyrighted music in the performance of this play and are strongly cautioned to do so. If no such permission is obtained by the licensee, then the licensee must use only original music that the licensee owns and controls. Licensees are solely responsible and liable for all music clearances and shall indemnify the copyright owners of the play(s) and their licensing agent, Samuel French, against any costs, expenses, losses and liabilities arising from the use of music by licensees. Please contact the appropriate music licensing authority in your territory for the rights to any incidental music.

IMPORTANT BILLING AND CREDIT REQUIREMENTS

If you have obtained performance rights to this title, please refer to your licensing agreement for important billing and credit requirements.